ORDERS

The Seacastle Mysteries
Book 6

PJ Skinner

ISBN 978-1-913224-53-0

Parkin Press
INDEPENDENT PUBLISHER

Cover design by Mariah Sinclair

Discover other titles by PJ Skinner

The Seacastle Mysteries

Deadly Return (Seacastle Mysteries Book 1)

Eternal Forest (Seacastle Mysteries Book 2)

Fatal Tribute (Seacastle Mysteries Book 3)

Toxic Vows (Seacastle Mysteries Book 4)

Mortal Vintage (Seacastle Mysteries Book 5)

Grave Reality (Seacastle Mysteries Book 7)

Purrfect Crime (A Christmas Mystery novella)

Mortal Mission A Mars Murder Mystery written as Pip Skinner

Green Family Saga (written as Kate Foley)
Rebel Green (Book 1)
Africa Green (Book 2)
Fighting Green (Book 3)

The Sam Harris Adventure Series (written as PJ Skinner)

Fool's Gold (Book 1)

Hitler's Finger (Book 2)

The Star of Simbako (Book 3)

The Pink Elephants (Book 4)

The Bonita Protocol (Book 5)

Digging Deeper (Book 6)

Concrete Jungle (Book 7)

Sam Harris Adventure Box Set Book 2-4

Sam Harris Adventure Box Set Book 5-7

Sam Harris Adventure Box Set Books 2-7

Also available as AI narrated audiobooks on YouTube and from my website

Go to the PJ Skinner website for more info and to purchase paperbacks and audiobooks directly from the author: https://www.pjskinner.com

Dedicated to my brother Rory

Emilie

Best wishes
from

Tanner.

Chapter 1

It had been raining for weeks, great sheets of water which hit the windows of the Grotty Hovel with evil intent. I spent my life mopping up leaks from the ill-fitting sash windows. At least the roof appeared to be sound. All over West Sussex, the rivers had broken their banks and invaded the houses built on their flood plains. Every night, broadcasts on the news channels showed sad owners wading through their sitting rooms among floating furniture. Seacastle had remained relatively unscathed by the deluge, but its soggy inhabitants had created their own tidal wave of complaints. The British weather had always provided a safe topic of conversation between strangers in the past, but vitriol normally directed at council tax and the bin men had spilled over into this genteel arena. I half expected someone to build an Ark at Shoreham, just in case.

As I slogged to work in my waterproofs, through yet another heavy shower, I muttered under my breath about moving to Spain or Greece before I went mouldy. The promenade was awash with water, which had run down the streets abutting it. The water never rose over an inch or two as it ran down through the pebble banks and into the sea, but I'd worn my wellies anyway to avoid water-logging my shoes. The Pavilion Theatre loomed through the rain like a giant grey barnacle guarding the entrance to the pier. I felt sorry for the businesses lurking along its length, waiting in vain for early season sunshine to bring in the punters. Seacastle has never been a Mecca for tourists, and the driving rain put off even the hardiest visitors. I turned on to King Street and headed north towards my vintage furniture shop, Second Home, which sat sullen and sodden on the High Street. Before going in, I turned left and walked the few paces to the Surfusion restaurant, also closed and dark.

I pressed my face up against the window and gazed in. The owners, Rohan Patel and Kieron Murphy, had made a fabulous job of decorating the interior, which resembled the bottom of a lagoon more than ever in the gloom. The interior had been painted in a sea green colour and furnished with painted chairs and tables. The cash desk had a seahorse motif, which was repeated on the doors to the toilets and the kitchen. The left-hand wall had been lined with taxidermy fish on a dark green background, decorated with painted kelp and seashells, protected by a thick glass cover. I had rescued the stuffed fish during the clearance of an old seadog's cottage near the Shanty pub, with my business partner and boyfriend, Harry Fletcher, so I felt partially responsible for the awesome effect. Finally, a small white soapstone statuette of Ganesha sat in an alcove over the door. I have given it to Surfusion for good luck, as Ganesha was the Hindu deity associated with new beginnings and the removal of obstacles. I hoped it would bring them good fortune as they were going to need it.

The owners of Surfusion had become a fixture in our circle since moving to Seacastle from Brighton at the suggestion of one of my closest friends, Ghita Chowdhury. She had helped them plan their menu and kept them from each other's throats as they fretted about the opening. Ghita had met Rohan on a blind date as part of her mother's vain attempt to find her a husband. After a rocky start, Ghita and Rohan had formed a close friendship; close enough to irritate Kieron, who suffered from fits of jealousy if Rohan even looked at another human. The three of them had formed an odd business ménage-à-trois, which mostly worked, but sometimes exploded into fighting and weeping. Ghita often took refuge with me until the storm had passed.

My eye was drawn to a small poster stuck at the bottom of the window. It announced the grand opening of the restaurant for the May Bank Holiday weekend. The opening of Surfusion had been postponed so often, I had thought it would never happen. It's not that I doubted their ability to pull it off. Despite my doubts about the wisdom of opening a high-end restaurant at the cheap end of Seacastle, they had persevered. Kieron had a wonderful palate and an imagination which rivalled Ghita's, and Rohan had the organisational skills Kieron lacked. It had not been smooth sailing. Kieron had been distracted by the death of his father, and the ensuing demands of his mother who had taken to her bed and insisted she too was moribund. Ghita struggled with her unrequited feelings for Rohan, and his exasperation with Kieron led to blazing arguments. However, it seemed as if they had finally lined all their ducks, or their fish, in a row.

I crossed the street, navigating the potholes full of murky water and walked the few metres to Second Home. The burgundy painted front streamed with water, which ran down the window, almost obscuring the display. I took out my keys and opened the door. The bell clanged in my ear as I entered, being careful not to tread water onto the post which lay on the floor. Soon my waterproofs lay in a damp pile, and I had changed into a pair of pixie boots I kept behind the counter. I hung the wet clothing on the coat hangers at the back of the shop and laid some paper on the floor underneath them to catch the drips. I climbed the stairs to the

Vintage Café and made myself a latte. I scrounged the last piece of almond shortbread from the cabinet and nibbled on it to make it last, feeling the golden crumbs melt on my tongue.

The coffee and shortbread gave me a new lease on life and I headed back downstairs to get started on the accounts. The rain had stopped, and the sun peeped through the clouds making the drops of water on the windows sparkle like crystals. I took out a stack of receipts and transferred them to the ledger using a basic calculator with a roll of paper to make running totals of the items. I glanced around at my depleted stock and decided to prod Harry to get us a house clearance soon. He had recently bought a second-hand van to replace his lamented former one, which he had inherited from his uncle. It had a larger capacity, and we were dying to try it out. I had asked my stepson, Mouse, to search online for an old-fashioned tape deck for the dashboard, as all of our best music still resided on cassettes. Yes, I'm still a closet Luddite.

The doorbell clanged, and Ghita bustled in on her habitual cloud of happiness and gave me a hug. Her eyes shone as she stood on her tiptoes to greet me. I wondered what new marvel she had dreamed up with her pals Rohan and Kieron that had caused her an almost manic level of excitement. Their combined creative natures produced a constant stream of delicious new dishes and exotic cake flavours, and I found it hard to keep up. I finished writing a number into the income column and stood up, rubbing the small of my back.

'That's me done for a bit,' I said. 'Do you fancy a cuppa?'

'Oh, yes, please. I've got amazing news. I can't wait to tell you.'

'I'd never have guessed.'

Ghita put on the kettle and I made myself a latte with the last of the milk. She produced a new batch of almond biscuits from her voluminous bag, which reminded me always of Hermione Granger's because of the random things she kept in it. I sat down with my coffee and took a nibble of one biscuit. Its crisp, buttery texture melted in my mouth and I sighed with ecstasy.

'Oh my, Miss Chowdhury. You have really outdone yourself this time. These are the nectar of the gods. They'll sell like hotcakes.'

Ghita reddened with pleasure.

'Rohan and I made them together. Well, um, it's not the only thing we're planning on making together.'

I arched an eyebrow.

'Come on. Spit it out. What evil treat are you two cooking up now?'

If I lived to be one hundred, I couldn't have guessed what she'd say next.

'You can't tell anyone, especially Roz, because, well, you know what she's like.'

I tried to imagine Roz broadcasting Ghita's new recipe all over Seacastle, but failed.

'Cross my heart.'

'We're going to make a baby.'

I dropped my cup on the floor. Luckily, it was empty, but it broke into several pieces. I swore under my breath and bent down to pick it up. Ghita perched on the edge of her chair, watching me, wringing her hands.

'Say something.'

'My flabber is ghasted to tell you the truth. I presume Kieron knows about this.'

Her expression changed.

'Not yet. Well, he's so busy with his mother. It didn't seem fair to, um. But Rohan's so excited.'

I sensed disaster. Kieron had already shown signs of jealousy where Ghita was concerned. I couldn't imagine how he would react if he had to share Rohan with a baby. But Ghita radiated joy, and I couldn't find a kind way to warn her. Instead, I hugged her and offered her more tea.

'When you say you're going to have a baby, are you pregnant already?' I asked.

'Oh, heavens no. We're still in the planning stages.'

I almost spat out my tea. Ghita claimed to be a virgin, something I found entirely plausible. Her few forays into the world of dating, mostly as a result of her mother's matchmaking, had not gone well. Ghita had standards. Not that there's anything wrong with having standards. But having 'Prince Charming on a white charger' standards, in a world full of Don Quixotes on donkeys, could be considered unrealistic at best. Her glib pronouncement told me she had not considered the mechanics at all. I swallowed my objections.

'Well, that's a wonderful idea, but perhaps you should wait until the restaurant has got established before you embark on your next project?'

'Of course, silly. You didn't think we'd do it right now, did you?'

Nothing would have surprised me, but I shook my head.

'I know you'll be thoughtful about this. Kieron has a lot to cope with right now. I don't think he could deal with baby talk.'

Ghita sighed.

'That's what Rohan said. Do you think I'm mad? I've never found anyone to love until I met Rohan. He's perfect, apart from being gay. And I love Kieron too, despite his hissy fits. They make me happy, and they love me too.'

'There's nothing more important than love. Just be careful. I don't want you getting hurt.'

'Pain is the price we pay for love.'

12

'It's too early for philosophy. Maybe we should have another cup of tea?'

Chapter 2

After closing the shop, I walked home along the promenade and stopped off at the wind shelter near my house to feed some crusts of bread to Herbert the seagull. He had sidled up to me as a young bird and shared my bacon sandwich while I had an impromptu picnic in the shelter on a windy day. Herbert had become a fixture in my life because of my habit of adopting animals and people into my circle. I also had a rescue cat at home, Hades, a black moggy with a white chest, expensive taste in cat food, and a serious attitude problem. They joined a long line of adoptees, including Mouse. He's the son of my ex-husband, DI George Carter, the offspring from his first marriage. Mouse's real name is Andrew Carter. He had moved into the Grotty Hovel uninvited when I got divorced and he has never left. We had become a team, and I loved him with all my heart.

Mouse had recently applied to study digital forensics at Portsmouth University in October and, having been accepted, he strained every sinew to earn money to support himself during the degree. He had been the centre of attention at the Vintage Café above Second Home since it had opened because of his Renaissance good looks; blue-grey eyes, alabaster skin and black curly hair. The female clientele adored him and I had no illusions about the effect his leaving for university would have on my turnover, or my heart. Kieron had offered him some shifts at the restaurant because of his experience running the café, and soon also had a willing helper to design the fish themed menus.

It began to drizzle again, and black clouds hung heavy over the wind farm. Choppy waves hit the pebble banks and mixed with the rainwater seeping through from the pavements. I slipped into the wind shelter and sat against the wall, blocking the wind and rain. I shivered despite the warm clothes under my waterproofs. Ghita's news had knocked me for six. I tried not to enter panic mode. Maybe Rohan and she would change their minds when they considered the implications of their plan. The fallout might be worse than they could deal with. Kieron had a tendency to overreact to the smallest upset. His reaction to his boyfriend having a baby without including him on the decision might be nuclear.

As I mused on their odd decision, a little girl shot past me on her bike, her plump pink legs shining wet as they whizzed around on the pedals. An older boy, probably her brother, followed her on another bike, closing the gap between them. Before I had time to worry about the speed they were going, the girl turned to look back at her brother, and simultaneously hit a bump on the pavement, almost stopping her bicycle in its tracks. She flew over the handlebars as my heart rose to my throat. Luckily, she didn't have far to fall, and had worn a safety helmet, so she was more shaken than hurt. Her father held her tight as she sobbed with fright. As I watched them cycle off in the rain, I wondered how parents could cope with the worry of something happening to their child. I hated Mouse staying out late, as I could never sleep until I heard his key in the lock, and I had only been his mother for just over a year. Ghita cried if one of her cakes didn't rise, or if someone was mean to her. How on earth would she deal with the fear of something happening to her child? Perhaps when she became a mother, she would develop a thicker skin.

Herbert skittered in on the wind and strutted up and down in front of me. I retrieved the crusts from the plastic bag and threw a few on the ground in front of him. He let loose some raucous cries and gobbled them up before anyone could pinch them. Seagulls seemed unable to keep a secret. If they found food, they yelled about it at top volume, even if it meant bigger stronger brethren would fly in and take it all. He had trouble swallowing the last bit, gulping and regurgitating the crust several times before it finally disappeared down his gullet. I could find no solutions for Ghita's troubles in the crashing waves and reminded myself that doom scrolling through so far non-existent problems solved nothing. I needed to get home and plan supper, so I hauled myself back into the wind and drizzle.

My small terraced house, known as The Grotty Hovel, sat on a road parallel to the promenade at three-minutes' walk from the shelter. I opened the front door with relief and stepped into the cosy interior, luxuriating in being surrounded by my favourite things, many of which had been purloined from my stock. Hades registered my presence and stalked away before I could try to stroke him. He sucked up to everyone else, but he never forgave me for rescuing him from the empty house next door. I had found him in a Lloyd Loom laundry basket and he seemed to think it had been my fault he got trapped in there. Mouse looked up from the chopping board in the kitchen and grinned at me.

'I'm making a fish pie,' he said. 'I used the leftover prawns, and a frozen fillet of haddock I found in the freezer. Can you help me make the white sauce? Last time mine came out lumpier than the seats in Harry's old van.'

'Of course. The trick is to keep stirring as quickly as you can while you add the milk. I'll show you. Any news from Harry?'

'No. He hasn't turned up yet.'

'I wonder what's keeping him?'

I took off my coat and dumped my handbag on the sofa and started the roux sauce for Mouse. His confidence in his cooking skills had increased exponentially since his first attempts, so I encouraged him with a combination of praise and tried and tested recipes. Like all of us, he enjoyed a takeaway, but his budget for university would not cover many of those. He would make a great housemate for someone with his newly acquired skills.

'How's it going at Surfusion?' I asked, expecting elaborate complaints about the constant hissy fits and chaos.

'It's okay,' he said, colour rising in his cheeks.

'Just okay?'

'Well, there's this girl who's come to work in the kitchen.'

I raised an eyebrow.

'And does this girl have a name?'

'Leanne.'

'What does she do there?'

'She runs the dishwasher and cleans the pots and pans. Sometimes she helps Kieron with the food prep. She's thinking of training to be a commis chef.'

'Do you like her?'

'Not like that. Not yet anyway. But she's funny, and she sticks up for herself when Kieron's being Kieron.'

'It's nice for you to have a friend in there. I realise it can get a little tense at times.'

'Ghita protects me from the worst spats. The atmosphere will get better after they open.'

'Definitely. It's hardly surprising they are on edge.'

The front door swung open and Harry's head popped around it.

'Ello, ello, ello. What's all this then?' he said, sniffing the air. 'I see we have a mouse in the kitchen again. That cat is useless.'

Hades did not raise his head from the sofa where he had climbed on top of my handbag to sleep.

'Are you coming in?' I said.

'Actually, I need you to come outside for a minute. Mouse too, if he can stop sweating over the hot stove.'

'I'm at the crucial stage of making a white sauce. Can I take a raincheck?'

'Okay, but you're missing out.'

Mystified, I followed Harry out onto the street and around the corner where he had parked his new van.

'Shut your eyes. I'll guide you,' he said, taking my hand.

It occurred to me he might have picked up a piece of furniture for me on his rounds, and I prepared to gasp in admiration. Unfortunately, his taste and mine were as far apart in vintage items as they were close in classic rock, but I always pretended to be thrilled. His heart was in the right place and that was far more important than his taste in furniture. I shuffled blindly along the pavement, clinging to his warm, calloused hand. Then, he stopped and took me by the shoulders, twisting me around to face the side of the van.

'Open your eyes.'

I did and blinked several times. The side of the van came into focus and with it a beautiful hand-painted sign – Bowe and Fletcher, Clearance Experts. Intricately detailed clematis vines and flowers surrounded the lettering. Tears filled my eyes, and I turned to him speechless. He searched my face for confirmation.

'Do you like it? My cousin Alf did it for us.'

'Like it?' I stuttered. 'It's so beautiful I don't have words.'

He swept me into his muscular embrace and kissed the tears from my eyes.

'Why are you crying, you silly goose?'

'I don't know. I'm emotional.'

'I can't get rid of you now. It's official.'

'I love you, Harry Fletcher.'

'Could you love me even more?'

'Why do you ask?'

'We've got a clearance tomorrow. It's a 60s era house with one owner.'

'I could. I do. Let's help Mouse with the fish pie. He'll be so excited to see the van.'

But he didn't move.

'Did you spot it?'

'Did I spot what?'

'Look at the sign again.'

And there among the vines framing the sign I saw it, a mouse. I felt my eyes filling again.

'Bring him out to see it. He'll be so excited,' I said.

'Can you guard the sauce?'

'I think I can manage that.'

Chapter 3

The next morning, we made the short drive to a row of terraced cottages off Seacastle High Street. The new van still felt alien to me, with its clean leatherette seats and digital dashboard. The friendly smell of old leather had been replaced by a slightly chemical odour, which made my nose wrinkle in protest. I missed the music too. We had always played our favourite cassette tapes in the old van. Mouse now wanted us to move into the twenty-first century and to use our phones for streaming. Harry refused to rely on a mast signal for his music or to pay for music he already owned. The so-called new van was actually ten years old, so it had a holder under the dashboard for a radio or tape deck. I had asked Mouse to scour the internet for one without telling Harry. I wanted to surprise him by having one installed.

I tapped my card on the parking meter while Harry pulled the van up to the kerb close to the cottage. The outside had recently been painted a pastel pink, which went with the others on the street. The row looked like a giant packet of sherbet Fizzers. Harry knocked on the door of the house, but nobody came to open it. He looked at his watch and tutted.

'Are you sure we've got the correct number?' I asked.

'Pretty sure,' said Harry, taking a crumpled piece of paper from his pocket and squinting at it.

I pressed my face against the window and tried to check the interior for interesting contents. The lace curtains obstructed my view, but I could see the outlines of cupboards and chairs which looked promising. Harry looked at his watch again. I resisted the temptation to tell him it was still ten-twenty-five, and the agent wasn't even late yet. I sympathised with anyone who came across Harry's almost psychotic punctuality. When we first got together my casual attitude to time keeping infuriated him. I had never looked at it from the other person's point of view before, but he had made me quite ashamed about how I expected people to wait for me. I had changed my ways and found I quite enjoyed being on time. No more last-minute panics or missed trains. I leaned against Harry and nuzzled his neck, making him go pink.

'Honestly, woman, there's a time and place,' he said, but he kissed me anyway.

A young man with bad acne and a suit two sizes too big for him interrupted our impromptu embrace. The look of horror on his face at finding two people his parents' age kissing made me smirk. I bet he thought we didn't do that anymore.

'Are you the ones who are doing the clearance?' he said, trying not to grimace.

'Yes, that's us,' said Harry.

'Will you leave the house empty?'

'It depends on the contents. We're not a charity.'

'I didn't think you were,' said the man, putting his key in the lock and opening the front door to a wonderland of Danish vintage furniture. I almost gasped. 'Is this the sort of thing you wanted?'

'I think we can find a home for it,' I said. 'What happened to the owners?'

'They died in a sailing accident.'

'That's terrible,' said Harry. 'Didn't they have any children?'

'Oh, yes, two I know of. The children gave us the order to sell the house and get rid of the contents. They already took the valuables away.'

'Were they Danish?' I asked.

'Only the wife, and they told me she wasn't their mother. I got the impression they hated her and wanted to get rid of all her things.'

'That's so sad,' I said.

He shrugged. An old shrug for such a young man.

'It happens. What time will you be finished?'

'Is there any more furniture upstairs?' asked Harry.

'Two bedrooms with similar blonde furniture.'

'Would you like me to call you?' I asked. 'It's hard to be sure when we'll finish.'

'No problem. I'm in and out all day, showing houses to clients. Just ping me and I'll come as soon as I can.'

'Why don't we lock up the house for you and you can come to my shop, Second Home, for a coffee and cake and collect the key at the same time?'

'Magic. Thanks. See you later.'

I watched him go, wondering how he could be so calm. I felt impotent with rage, but Harry put his hand on my shoulder.

'You don't know the complete story. Maybe their father dumped their mother for his second wife. Maybe she mistreated them or made them leave home. Don't judge. Just be happy with our haul.'

I took a deep breath and released it slowly, feeling the tension in my back decrease. Harry did not appear to be a sensitive man, but still waters run deep, cavernous in his case. I smiled at him.

'You're right. This looks exciting.'

'It looks pretty dull to me. What's so good about it?'

'These pieces were made by Danish designers in the 60s and 70s. Some of them are now worth a lot of money, but I don't know which ones until I look them up.'

'But you want them all.'

'Absolutely.'

'Let's get lifting then.'

It took us several hours to empty the house, taking the vintage pieces first and unloading them at the shop. Mouse received the booty with glee, his fingers itching to surf the internet and attribute makers to each piece. The second van load comprised random pieces of IKEA and modern soft furnishings I wouldn't be able to sell in my shop. The new van had a greater capacity than the old one, which made it both more and less useful for different reasons. Even so, we only just managed to fit everything into the back.

'Tommy will be thrilled with this lot,' said Harry, stretching his back. 'There's some good quality here in mint condition.'

Harry's cousin Tommy was only one of a vast network of his relatives, who lived mostly in the East End of London. The only other relation I had met so far was Harry's brother Nick, who had recently moved to Devon. They had made up after being estranged for years and begun rebuilding their relationship.

'When will you deliver it?' I said.

'I might as well do it today. I'll call him and check if it's okay to pitch up this afternoon. Let's have a coffee at the Vintage and I'll set out.'

Mouse welcomed us back to the shop, his eyes gleaming with excitement.

'You'll never guess how much some of these pieces are worth.'

'Can we have our coffee first?' said Harry. 'Pleasure before business.'

Mouse deflated and squirmed with impatience, but I shook my head at him. Despite being ex-army, Harry rarely gave an order, but I liked to respect it when he did.

When we had finished, Mouse tidied away the cups and brought his laptop over to the table.

'I'm off,' said Harry, getting up.

Mouse's face fell.

'Don't you want to know about the values? It's amazing.'

Harry smiled.

'If it's alright with my business partner, I'd like to buy you a new laptop for your degree with my share. I imagine you'll need something high-powered and expensive for all that crypto science?'

I thought Mouse might cry. He bit his lip and his eyes became moist.

'Really?' he said. 'It's a lot of money.'

'I expect you to keep me in my old age, in the style to which I'd like to become accustomed.'

Mouse gave Harry a fierce hug. Harry became quite pink with pleasure and embarrassment.

'Is that okay with you?' asked Mouse.

I nodded.

'Bang goes my holiday in the Caribbean.'

'Not necessarily,' said Mouse. 'You haven't seen these prices yet.'

Chapter 4

The welcome news about the value of our clearance gave me a second wind, and, after Harry had left, I started to polish and clean the stock. I placed the best pieces, a set of six wood and leather dining chairs by Niels Møller, in the window display. I often did this as a ploy to attract the competition, Grace Wong and her husband Max who ran a high-end antique shop down at the posh end of the high street. However, Grace did not sell vintage furniture, no matter the quality, so they were unlikely to interest her. The catch for whom I had dangled the bait were the newly arrived refugees from the high prices of housing in Brighton. Seacastle properties were half the price of its wealthy neighbour, meaning that anyone from there who bought a house in Seacastle often had money to burn. They could afford to spend more money on furnishings, and luckily for Rohan and Kieron, on dining out. I had fretted for months over the wisdom of opening a high-end fusion restaurant in our town, but the influx of these residents had doubled the prospects for success. They thought nothing of spending far more than locals would on what Ghita referred to as 'an exclusive dining experience'.

I had Mouse working on a new project, a vintage shop on eBay, featuring our best pieces to widen the net for prospective clients. Collectors of classic Danish furniture would travel many miles to pick up a signature piece, so it made sense to advertise them online. Mouse had assured me it would be simple to run, but I had my doubts. Processes that came easily to him seemed like labyrinths of complexity to me. I used anglepoise lamps to illuminate each item and snapped photographs for the website, as well as taking their measurements. Mouse uploaded the information to a shop page and showed me the results of his labour. We chose 'buy now' and minimum prices and set the auctions rolling. I breathed a sigh of relief when we had finished. Damp patches under my arms spoke volumes about the stress I experienced. Mouse noticed and rolled his eyes at me.

'Honestly,' he said. 'You're not on death row. You're selling some second-hand furniture.'

Before I could come up with an amusing retort, the doorbell rang, and Rohan entered.

'Ah, there you are Mouse. Can you please help Kieron with the menus? Ed couldn't source any scallops for one of our dishes because of a large order from Tarton Manor House. Kieron is going berserk about the late change in the menu. He's not the only one. I might have a conniption if we have to change them again.'

Mouse grinned.

'I'll deal with it. Stay here and have a nice hot beverage with Tanya until your heart rate returns to normal.'

'Do you mind?' said Rohan. 'I'm not disturbing you, am I?'

'Of course not,' I said. 'I'm due a break. Let's go upstairs.'

I followed Rohan upstairs, admiring his burgundy velvet suit. His jet-black hair had been oiled into place and his moustache waxed into stiff curls. Rohan always made me feel frumpy as I went for comfort-first clothing options. I wished I had the same fashion sense. He smelled good too. Like grapefruit and spices.

'That's a great cologne. What is it?'

'Dior Sauvage Elixir.'

'Did Kieron give it to you?'

He snorted.

'Kieron is a cheapskate. He'd buy me Versace if I let him.'

'What can I get you?'

'Can I have a jasmine tea please?'

I made a big pot for both of us. Grace had given me some of her private stash. The fragrant smell mixed with Rohan's cologne. He raised his cup to his lips and sniffed.

'Oh my, that's special. We need some of that for Surfusion.'

'You may have to murder Grace to get your hands on it.'

'If Machiavelli owned a restaurant…'

'Anyway, how's it going over there? Are you ready for the big night?'

'Physically, yes, everything is in place. Mentally, I'm not at all sure. Kieron is being impossible, and Ghita is at the end of her tether.'

I looked at him over the rim of my cup. His handsome face was drawn, and he had bags under his eyes.

'You're fond of her, aren't you?'

He lifted his head to gaze into my eyes and despite my feigned innocence, he sighed at what he saw there.

'She told you. She shouldn't have done that. Kieron doesn't know yet.'

'About the baby? Yes. She tells me everything. Um, have you thought about this? I mean, really thought about the consequences?'

'Of course we have. We haven't made a final decision yet. I have to discuss it with Kieron first.'

I didn't remember Ghita being in any doubt, but I let it go.

'How do you think he'll take it?'

Rohan sighed.

'Kieron's jealous. He's jealous of my socks because they're touching my feet. It's almost pathological. I'm not sure how he'd react about sharing me with a baby.'

'Even if it was his?'

Rohan's cheek muscles tightened.

'I hadn't thought of that. I hoped to be a father myself.'

'You need to talk to him after the restaurant opens, and before you go any further with this plan.'

'I know. I'm just so desperate for a family. That's why I agreed to meet Ghita in the first place. My family doesn't know I'm gay.'

'But how—'

'The only one who knows is my brother, Krish, and he's sworn to secrecy.'

'I didn't know you had a brother. Can you trust him to keep your secret?'

'I used to think so. Only, he's been threatening to tell my parents recently and I don't know what to do.'

I had no idea how to deal with this revelation. Did he want me to suggest something? I felt completely out of my depth in the conversation. Ghita's parents had turned out to be surprisingly tolerant of her odd arrangement with Rohan and Kieron. Her mother had been happy to see Ghita so contented, and her father enjoyed his ignorance as long as his wife didn't complain. Ghita had looked after her maternal grandparents until their deaths and had inherited their flat in Seacastle. This gave her financial independence and had removed control from her parents. They had little option other than accepting her choices, and, despite appearances,

Ghita was no pushover. He wrung his hands together and sighed.

'I assume your parents don't know about Kieron. How long have you been going out together?'

'Not that long, officially. Only a year or so.'

He picked at a thread hanging from the sleeve of his jacket and showed no intention of elaborating.

'And unofficially?'

'He courted me after I came to the restaurant where he worked in Brighton. He already had a boyfriend, but that didn't stop him. I fell under his spell. Kieron can be irresistible when he puts his mind to it.'

'And the boyfriend?'

'Dumped without a backwards glance. Kieron is ruthless.'

'But you love him?'

'Passionately. Or I did. The stress of opening the restaurant has made us both tetchy and intolerant.'

'Hang in there. Things will go back to normal after the opening night.'

'Or until I tell him about the baby,'

Chapter 5

The conversation I'd had with Rohan weighed heavily on my mind over the next few days. I couldn't imagine how he coped with the pressure. How did he deal with all his conflicting emotions? I wanted to discuss it with someone who might suggest how I could help, but who could offer advice? Unlike Brighton, Seacastle's nascent gay community had not come out loud and proud yet. Miles Quirk was the only other gay man I knew, and I doubted he would consider me as a friend after the saga of the Seacastle coven. I kept him in reserve in case of emergencies.

As the days went by, my dilemma remained unresolved. I had my work cut out running the Vintage, and serving in the shop, without Mouse or Ghita. Roz Murray, my other stalwart friend, hadn't been available either. She'd been out at sea with her fisherman husband, Ed, helping him to check their traps. The Murrays had concentrated on using static gear like lobster pots after a Marine Protection Area had been implemented offshore at Seacastle and using nets had been banned. Despite fierce competition, they had taken over a corner of the restaurant and hotel market for crabs and lobsters. They had also snared the Surfusion account, which made Roz crow with triumph. This had not gone down well with the fishermen from Shoreham, whose former monopoly on the supply of expensive crustaceans to local restaurants had been broken.

My stock of Danish vintage furniture had been reduced quicker than I had imagined. Our eBay page had been a success, and I had a visit from a London dealer who snapped up the Neils Møller chairs and a sideboard without a quibble on the price. Other pieces were still under auction and had healthy bids increasing on them. New technology, new for me anyway, never failed to impress me. My former reluctance to use it had dissipated with every foray into a new application and I wondered why I had waited so long to enter the modern era. I had initially been worried about security, but Mouse had made sure I had decent firewalls to keep out hackers like him. I wondered how I would fare once he had gone to university. I could imagine panicked phone calls were going to become a common occurrence once he had left the Grotty Hovel for Portsmouth.

Before I knew it, Surfusion's opening night had arrived. Mouse set out early for the restaurant, dressed in a pair of new black polyester trousers and a white shirt. He had washed his hair and his black curls formed a devastating curtain around his handsome face. He still looked too young to have a job, but you know what they say about policemen as you get older. Harry and I got dressed up after a shower. I wore my favourite blue shiny body sheath dress, which contained enough Lycra to adapt to over-eating of delicious food. Harry wore his slacks and an old corduroy jacket. Except for his bald head, he looked like Harrison Ford about to lecture to his history class. I found it quite alluring. Hades kept trying to sit on his lap and pin him to the sofa. He had covered the entire house in a carpet of shed fur since he had started moulting for the summer. I distracted him with some pieces of cold chicken.

Against my better judgement, I had invited Helen and George to come to the opening with us. My sister Helen had recently divorced her husband and, to the astonishment of all, she had been courted by and hooked up with George, my ex-husband. I know people found it strange, but I didn't mind about them getting together. I didn't love him anymore, and they were like two peas in a pod. I'm a great believer in fate and their love felt like that to me. Helen had been in a high state of excitement for ages, calling me twice a day to consult me on her outfit choices. George took a dim view of the whole idea of fusion cuisine, but I suspected he had never tried it. He searched for an excuse not to go, but Helen ignored his pleas. She had no intention of going without him. Flo, the local pathologist, had also been invited, but she had come down with flu and had been confined to her bed. She made me promise to give her a rundown of the whole evening and bring her a menu to peruse in her sickbed.

George picked us up in his saloon car and drove us along the promenade. The full moon projected a silver road which ran from the horizon to the pebbled shore. I gazed at it, wondering what would happen if I followed it. Would it be like the yellow brick road or would there be less singing? We parked so far from the restaurant that my high heels gave me blisters. They were not built for walking, only posing. I bit back my complaint. There was zero point starting the night off by whinging. As we approached the restaurant, we could see a queue of people waiting to get in. From the way they were dressed, I guessed they had expected a night club. Poor old Mouse was at the door turning them away. I quite enjoyed waltzing past them into the underwater emporium. The smell of spices hit my sinuses with a powerful punch as we entered. I whispered a salutation to the statuette of Ganesha, who sat in his own alcove above the door, welcoming the guests and blessing the new venture.

Rohan rushed up to us, his cheeks pink with excitement.

'You'll never guess what,' he said. 'Leonard Black is coming. The Leonard Black!'

I had no idea who that was. The only show I watched with any regularity was Sloane Rangers with Mouse, and that was only because he had a crush on Daisy Kallis. I looked to Helen for guidance. She was my guru on matters of fame as she watched soap operas and reality shows, and loved gossip on social media. But she shrugged.

'Search me.'

Rohan snorted.

'I can't believe none of you know who Black is,' said Rohan. 'He's the most famous restaurant critic in Britain. His reviews can make or break a restaurant.'

'And he's coming here tonight?' I asked. 'What does he look like?'

'That's just it. Nobody knows. He's an enigma. Normally he comes in and eats without you ever realising he has been.'

'So how do you know he's coming?' said George.

Rohan tapped the side of his nose with his index finger.

'He rang and asked for a reservation.'

'Not so secret then,' I said.

Rohan appeared hyper rather than nervous. The extra stress of having someone like Leonard Black turning up had taken him to the brink of hysteria.

'Does Kieron know?' said Harry.

Rohan put his finger to his lips.

'Of course not. He wouldn't be able to cope. I'll tell him after I've read the review.'

'When will it be published?' I asked.

'He does them straight away, sometimes while he's still in the restaurant.'

'Where does he post them?' said Helen.

'I'll send you the link if it's good,' said Rohan. 'Let me take you to your table.'

He seated us at the back of the restaurant where we could watch everything that went on. Harry pulled out my chair, and I sat beside Helen so we could share each other's food. We had similar taste, being sisters, and enjoyed choosing dishes we both liked. George rolled his eyes at this arrangement.

'Honestly, we're not in kindergarten now. Harry and I are the only adults at our table,' he said.

Harry patted George on the shoulder in solidarity, but he winked at me too. I looked around at the restaurant, taking in the excited faces of people gazing at the wall of fish and their menus, and unwrapping their heavy linen napkins, which had been folded to look like seashells. The thick nap of our tablecloth felt heavy on my legs. The clink of glasses, the scraping of chairs and the popping of a cork were interspersed with the rising sound of conversation. The smell of spice I had picked up on my entrance had mingled with the many perfumes and colognes worn by the clients. My stomach rumbled, reminding me of my decision to skip lunch to ensure my appetite would be ravenous. Having seen the size of the portions I wasn't convinced this had been the best option. I ate a sesame cracker in the shape of a scallop. It melted in my mouth in delicate saltiness and I suspected Ghita's hand in its production.

Mouse brought us our menus and took our drinks order. He had switched to work mode and his professional manner and smart clothes startled me. I glimpsed Ghita carrying out a tray of starters. She had worn her best sari, and she looked stunning in bright pink, with her long, dark brown hair hanging down her back in a single plait. She gave me a slightly harried looking smile before handing out the meals to the clients. Oohs and aahs accompanied her descriptions and the first tastes of the exquisite morsels. George frowned as he watched the performance.

'Those are starters? Are they feeding elves?'

Harry laughed.

'Wait until you read the menu. What's a heritage tomato? Is it a fossil of some sort?'

'A balsamic reduction sounds like something a judge would do to a prison sentence.'

They both chortled.

'Have you seen the prices?' said Harry.

George turned purple with suppressed annoyance.

'They've got a damn cheek charging an arm and a leg for those tiny dishes.'

'It must be the heritage tomatoes,' I said, trying to lighten the mood.

'Inheritance tomatoes more like it,' said Harry.

'Lettuce not make a fuss,' said Helen.

'Enough of the corny jokes,' I said. 'I'll tell Ghita not to shrimp on our portions.'

'I'll stop being crabby then,' said George, and we all laughed.

Humour having been restored, we ordered and sat back to observe the scene and play guessing games about who might be Leonard Black. In the end, we didn't need to guess. He swept in wearing a black cloak with a red lining ('like a magician' whispered Helen) and a black fedora with a red band and posed in the doorway theatrically while a flustered Rohan took them from him. He tried to guide Black to a table in the window. Black shook his head and pointed to one near us, in the corner beside the toilets. Rohan's face betrayed his dismay at the choice, but he nodded. Black stopped on his way to the corner to gaze at the taxidermy fish and stroke his black goatee. He arrived at his table and sat down.

'He's wearing a wig,' said Helen.

'A rug?' said Harry, rubbing his own bald head. 'Why would anyone bother? He must be sweating underneath all that hair.'

Both Black's jet-black hair and goatee were flecked with silver, but his face appeared unwrinkled. He did not smile at anyone on the adjoining tables. He shook out his napkin so that the folds unravelled before placing it in his lap and then picking up the menu.

'Let the games begin,' said Harry.

Chapter 6

Despite George's strong prejudice against fusion cuisine as 'merely an excuse to serve miniscule portions to people who didn't know any better', even he declared himself blown away by the first course. The combination of the fresh seafood and innovative flavours made every mouthful a feast for the senses.

'Oh my goodness! This is pure heaven on a plate,' said Helen. 'These prawns are delicious.'

'These salmon parcels are so unusual,' said Harry. 'I could eat a whole plateful of them, not just three.'

I wiped my mouth to remove a drop of sticky balsamic and ginger reduction and sneaked a look at Leonard Black. He had received his starter and had lifted a forkful to his mouth, which he sniffed before putting it in his mouth. He chewed it slowly, shutting his eyes. I couldn't tell if he liked it or not, as his expression didn't change. Helen offered me a prawn, which I took, and savoured. It was indeed heaven on a fork. From the ecstatic expressions on the faces of the other diners, the cooking had hit the spot at other tables too. I noticed Rohan allow himself a nervous fist pump below the cash desk. I wondered how Ghita and Kieron were getting on in the kitchen. Surely the success of the evening would heal some rifts in their relationship? Kieron had been sullen and even surly with me when I had greeted him in the street the day before the opening. I had assumed the pressure of opening the restaurant had got to him and had not taken it to heart.

Leonard Black patted his pockets and removed a mobile phone. He did some scrolling as if he had expected to receive an important message. He scratched his head and frowned. Then he placed it on the table beside his knife. I assumed he would type his review in there, but he pulled out a notebook instead. He took a small pencil out of the spine, licking the tip before drawing something. Would he make notes to inform his review? I couldn't see any writing. He shut the notebook again and laid it down beside his plate, his expression neutral. Mouse approached his table and asked permission to remove his empty plate. Black nodded condescendingly, which I knew would raise Mouse's hackles. Mouse did not react, but took the plate into the kitchen and soon emerged with the main course, which he set down in front of Black with exaggerated care.

'Didn't we order before that man?' said George.

'Perhaps world-famous restaurant critics get priority on opening night,' said Helen, patting his arm.

'That's the critic? I thought he might be Flo's brother.'

He had a point. Flo also had a flair for the dramatic and wore a similar cloak over her often flamboyant outfits. She also had black hair flecked with grey, which she wore in an always chaotic bun. Harry snorted, but I dug him in the ribs and he refrained from commenting. Ghita came over with our main courses and handed them around.

'Has everything tasted okay?' she said, pale with tension.

'Fabulous,' said Harry. 'I've never had better.'

A smile ghosted across Ghita's face. She glanced at Black.

'Can you tell if he likes his food or not?' she asked.

'Not really. He's not giving anything away,' I said.

Then I noticed Black beckoning Ghita over to his table and alerted her with a nudge. She approached him with caution, as if he might bite, and stood chewing her lip as she listened to him, her cheeks reddening. He handed her his plate, and she carried it towards the kitchen, her shoulders drooping as if in anticipation of a tongue lashing from Kieron.

'He hasn't eaten his food,' said George. 'Is that a bad sign?'

'I don't know what happened there. Surely he can't be rejecting it?' said Helen.

'I'm not sure,' I said. 'His plate was only half empty. I hope it doesn't spell disaster.'

Then Black's phone pinged, and he read his message. His eyebrows flew up, and he shook his head before appearing to delete it. He stood up and walked into the men's toilet. I noticed he took the phone with him. I wondered if he planned to write a review in there, out of sight. It didn't seem likely, but who knew? Maybe he wanted to be sure nobody would read it. I crossed my fingers he had not found fault with Kieron's cooking. His visit seemed less serendipitous and more calamitous at every turn.

Black took a while to emerge, so we lost interest and tucked into our food with exclamations of appreciation. I tried not to think about Black's apparent rejection of the food or Ghita's expression as she walked back to the kitchen. I'm not sure I've ever tasted anything as delicious as the lightly curried sauce which accompanied my fillet of plaice. If I hadn't been in the restaurant, I would have licked my plate. I ran a finger around the rim and sucked it. Helen tutted.

'Do you have to?' she said. 'We're not savages.'

I rolled my eyes at her and sneaked another glance at Black. He had received a second main course and new cutlery from Mouse. He savoured the first mouthful slowly and then ate the rest of the meal with vigour, clearing his plate and wiping it with a morsel of bread. He dabbed his mouth with his napkin and made another entry in his notebook. Mouse, who had been hovering at the cash desk, removed Black's empty plate and offered him a coffee, which he accepted with a tight smile.

Mouse disappeared into the kitchen. Seconds later, I heard the loud crash of something metallic and loud shouting. It sounded like Kieron blowing a fuse about something. Then Rohan could also be heard yelling back at him or with him, I wasn't sure. Black turned to look towards the kitchen door and raised his eyebrows. I held my breath. He shook his head and wiped his mouth with exaggerated care. Finally, Mouse emerged again, his jaw muscles working. He took an espresso coffee and a selection of almond biscuits over to the critic's table. He placed them in front of Black without smiling, which was most unlike him. I wondered what on earth had happened in the kitchen. I beckoned Mouse over to our table. Mouse came over to us, his face like thunder. He leaned over and whispered into my ear.

'The critic's review is up, and it's a stinker. All hell has broken out in the kitchen. Kieron is breaking things, Ghita is crying and Rohan is catatonic. I'm the only one still standing.'

'But how can that be?' I asked. 'Black ate everything on his plate and he's sitting calmly at his table nibbling on his biscuits. I think he's even smiling.'

'Smirking perhaps?' said Mouse. 'When people read his review, it will ruin the restaurant. Nobody will come here once they've read it.'

'It's that bad?' I said, sucking air through my teeth. 'What a disaster.'

'What's a disaster?' said Helen. 'What have I missed?'

A high-pitched scream echoed through the restaurant. As I looked around to find the cause of the commotion, the critic slid off his chair, his hands to his throat, appearing to choke. He pulled the linen tablecloth and all the items on the table down with him. His half-full coffee cup bounced on the floor twice before shattering, leaving a stain spreading across the cream-coloured tablecloth. Black lay contorted on the floor, trying to speak, but no sound emerged. His wig had become detached and hung from his head, revealing a thatch of brown hair. I didn't have time to consider this odd sight before he became still, his mouth and eyes wide in terror. George jumped up and ran straight over to him, surprising me with his agility. He pulled at Black's cravat and undid the buttons on his shirt. Then he started chest compressions. It appeared to be a waste of time, but George didn't falter.

'I need an EpiPen. Now!'

Mouse ran to the kitchen.

'And call an ambulance,' he shouted at me, red in the face with exertion.

I took out my phone and dialled the emergency services. I asked for an ambulance, and the police as well, to cover all bases. I had a nasty feeling creeping up my spine. Mouse emerged from the kitchen shaking his head. George looked around in desperation.

'Try his cloak. If he has allergies, it might be in the pocket.'

Mouse ran through the tables of horrified customers to where Black's cloak hung on the coat-stand. He patted it down. Sure enough, he found a pen and ran back to George's side with it. George took off the top and jammed it into Black's upper thigh. Ghita, Kieron and Rohan came out of the kitchen behind Mouse. Ghita's hand flew to her mouth when she spotted the body. Kieron turned as white as a sheet. They tried to approach Black, but George stopped them.

'Get back into the kitchen now,' he shouted at the shocked owners. 'Don't come out until I call you again.'

He continued to give chest compressions to the prostrate man, but Black did not respond. His head lolled on his neck. George lifted it from the floor, placing it on a seat cushion and put the body in recovery position. Black's lifeless eyes stared straight ahead, and foam had gathered at the corners of his mouth. He looked dead to me.

'I think you'll need to call Flo too,' said Mouse.

'But she's got the flu.'

'PC Brennan anyway. In case he's been poisoned,' said Mouse, avoiding my gaze.

'Whatever makes you say that?' said Helen.

'Kieron was swearing he would kill Black about ten minutes ago. I had no idea he meant it, or I would have done something.'

'Don't jump to conclusions,' I said. 'He may have had a seizure or a heart attack.'

'Maybe we should cordon the place off, just in case?' said Harry to George.

George sighed and nodded. He stood up and took out his warrant card, and they cleared the restaurant. They met no resistance. People had already moved towards the door. Mouse bent over the body. George shook his head.

'Don't touch him. It may be a crime scene now,' he said. 'The man is finished.'

Ghita gasped and clutched at Rohan, who had frozen on the spot with horror instead of going into the kitchen.

'And so is our restaurant,' he said. 'If we poisoned him, Surfusion's first night will be its last.'

Chapter 7

George asked Joe Brennan to drive us home while he waited for the forensics team and tried to get somebody to certify the death of Leonard Black. Joe, who worked on George's team at the station, had become a firm favourite with us for his cheery character and steel resolve. I tried to make conversation with him to dispel the tension in the car.

'I hear you passed the sergeant's exams with flying colours. We'll need to call you DS Brennan from now on,' I said. 'Will you try for inspector next?'

'Thanks. George has me on the fast-track programme. I should get the chance of promotion within the next two years.'

'That's brilliant. He could use some help around here.'

'I reckon he's doing okay with his unofficial assistant.'

He smirked at me. Nobody who worked at Seacastle police station was unaware of George's reliance on my interference in his cases. Being the ex-wife of the Detective Inspector represented a training in itself.

Joe delivered Harry and me to the Grotty Hovel and then continued on with Helen who refused an invitation to stay with us. She showed all the signs of being overwrought and needing a quiet time to sort her head out. Mouse had stayed behind at Surfusion to do an interview about his immediate recollections of the incident. He told me later that George kept Ghita, Leanne, Rohan and Kieron waiting in the kitchen while forensics scoured the scene for evidence. Everyone on the staff had been fingerprinted 'to eliminate them from enquiries'. I recognised this as a favourite technique of his; letting people stew while they imagined what tales the evidence might be telling. Apparently, Kieron had been hysterical with fury and frustration over the incident. He didn't seem to realise that as the chef, he had direct access to the food that could have been responsible for Black's demise. Mouse had showed George the awful review which had been posted on the critic's blog. It alone gave Rohan and Kieron a powerful motive for killing Black.

Flo had offered to crawl out of bed to certify the death, but Donald Friske, her counterpart in Brighton, had been co-opted against his will. He turned up in a high dudgeon, dressed in a dinner jacket and muttering under his breath. His first impression had been that Black had been poisoned, but Mouse had spotted an inhaler on the floor close to the body, which muddied the waters somewhat. It had been packaged up by the forensic team as evidence. I recalled Black putting his hands to his throat in panic, as if he couldn't breathe. Unexpected deaths were not always murders. Perhaps he had been allergic to something? It could have been poison, but I had seen him eat the ceviche, and I had eaten it too, with no ill effects.

The next morning, news of the death of Leonard Black at Surfusion spread like wildfire and stunned the whole of Seacastle. It was the only topic of conversation in the town's hairdressers, bars and coffee shops. People were agog at the horrible occurrence and those who had been at the restaurant at the time milked their experience for all it was worth. I didn't feel like going to work at all, but staying at home and brooding would have been worse. Mouse and I had a subdued breakfast together before setting out towards the promenade. We grunted at each other as we assembled bacon butties and made a pot of tea.

After we finished, Mouse washed up, and I packed some old pieces of bacon rind and crusts of bread in a plastic bag to give to Herbert the herring gull. Mouse rolled his eyes when he saw my offering.

'Honestly, he doesn't even know you. He's just an opportunist who sees you as a sucker.'

'That's not true. Seagulls remember people who give them food. That's why they're so successful.'

'Who told you that?'

'Google.'

'Huh. Maybe he recognises a sucker when he sees one.'

I punched his arm, but he just laughed at me.

'Come on, slugger. Herbert will be waiting.'

I slipped my arm through his and pulled him closer to me. He didn't try to escape. Mouse thrived on affection after his lonely childhood, and I had a boundless love for him. We walked in lockstep to the shelter and had hardly sat down before Herbert glided in and plopped down on his pink feet in front of us. He cocked his head at me and shuffled to one side of the shelter, avoiding getting too near to Mouse. I undid the bag and threw him the bacon rinds and crusts which he gobbled up with glee, the red spot on his bright yellow beak bobbing. When he had finished, he lifted his wings and caught the breeze up into the sky. We watched him go without thinking of leaving yet. Mouse turned to me.

'What do you think happened last night?' he said. 'I've gone over the whole evening in my head many times, but I can't find any explanation.'

'I don't know. Well, that's not true. I have many of them. I just can't imagine that any of them hold water.'

Mouse put his head in his hands and sighed.

'It's my fault, really. He died because of me.'

I couldn't believe what I was hearing.

'How can you say that?'

'I showed Kieron the review. I didn't mean to, but he saw my face when I found it. He forced me to show it to him. I've never seen anyone so angry. He threw a tray against the wall and screamed until he went purple. Ghita hid behind Rohan, but he got mad too and shouted at Kieron. I didn't know what to do.'

'That doesn't make it your fault. Leonard Black may be dead, but it could have been an allergy or a heart attack. Nobody is calling this murder yet.'

'But what if somebody poisoned him?'

'Do you really think Kieron or Rohan kept a bottle of poison handy in the kitchen in case of critical reviews? This isn't a tv show.'

Mouse couldn't help smiling.

'It could be, though. It's such a cliché killing the restaurant critic. It's a real Jessica Fletcher moment.'

'We can't be sure somebody killed him. So far, all we know is that he died. It wasn't pretty, but nobody has any proof of murder either. Do you remember what they were shouting about?'

'They were blaming each other for the review, I think. I don't remember it clearly. I had to calm Ghita down, so we could take the coffee and biscuits to Mr Black.'

'What time did the review appear?'

'I'm not sure. I can check the timestamp.'

'Why don't you do that and we'll make a timeline in Second Home just for us?'

'George won't like it. He told me you're not to get involved.'

'He always says that. Anyway, I don't care. Three of our friends are implicated in this affair, and even if they are not involved, they spent all of their savings on the Surfusion. If it goes bankrupt, Ghita will be devastated. We can't let that happen. I'll let George know if we discover anything he hasn't already found out.'

'Okay. It's a deal.'

We stood up and walked along the front to the shop. The tide was out, and the sun glinted off the rock pools. A man and his dog played fetch with a tennis ball, or at least tried to. The dog did not seem to understand the bit about bringing the ball back. They were larking about, splashing through the puddles of seawater together without a care in the world. I wondered how Hades would cope if I introduced a new pet into the Grotty Hovel. His face, sullen with disapproval, floated into my mind's eye. It made me guffaw, and Mouse looked at me strangely.

We crossed the promenade into King Street and headed towards the High Street. As we emerged from the wind tunnel formed by the street, we both looked left towards Surfusion. Yellow police tape had been stuck across the door and a notice forbidding entry affixed on the glass. The interior was dark. I couldn't see the statuette of Ganesha in the alcove. Its absence worried me. It seemed as if good luck had abandoned Surfusion and left it desolate. I wondered where Rohan and Kieron were. They couldn't have had a wink of sleep. I wondered if they had talked about what had happened yet, without screaming at each other. What on earth would they do now? How would they salvage the reputation of their brainchild?

To my surprise, Ghita stood outside Second Home, desolate and haggard. Her hair had escaped from its plait, and she still wore her special pink sari under her coat. She let out a loud sob as we approached and flung herself into my arms, dripping bitter tears all down my front. I passed Mouse the key so he could open up the shop. He shoved the door hard to move the mail, which always got jammed under it. I helped Ghita indoors. Her wobbly legs only held her that far, and she collapsed into the nearest chair with a heartfelt groan.

'We're ruined. What are we going to do?'

'I wouldn't go that far,' I said, lying. 'This is a temporary setback.'

Her eyes opened wide at this statement.

'How can you say that? A man died of poison in our restaurant on our opening night. How do we recover from that?'

I noticed she called Surfusion 'our restaurant', but I didn't comment. She had also put a massive effort into making it a success.

'There's zero reason to believe that he was poisoned,' I said. 'He may have had a heart attack,' I said. 'Anyway, people have short memories.'

'There's no such thing as a short memory since the invention of the internet,' said Mouse.

I glared at him to make him keep his opinions to himself, and he shrugged at me. Ghita sat up straighter and put her handbag on her lap.

'And the review? Are you forgetting the review?' she said.

I sighed.

'That's true,' I said. 'I had forgotten about it.'

'That review will live forever on the internet, long after the restaurant is gone,' said Mouse, unhelpfully I thought.

'There's no use crying over spilt milk,' I said, going for another cliché to fill the gap. 'First, we need to find out what happened to Leonard Black. Then we can deal with the review.'

Ghita reached inside her bag and took out the statuette of Ganesha, which she thumped down on the counter.

'Here, take it. You're going to need all the luck you can get.'

Chapter 8

I sent Ghita home to get some sleep and Mouse to buy us milk from the Co-op for the coffee. I kept reliving the awful scene at Surfusion as Leonard Black fell to the ground grabbing his throat, and George doing fruitless chest compressions as he choked. And then I remembered Black's wig falling off to reveal a head of brown hair underneath. Why would anyone with that much hair wear a wig? Perhaps he didn't want anyone to take a photograph and try to identify him. He had prided himself on his anonymity, like the Banksy of food critics. His entire image seemed designed to keep him hidden from view, despite his public persona. An enigma wrapped inside a riddle.

While I waited for Mouse to come back, I carried out an internet search on Leonard Black. Web pages, full of speculation about his real identity, competed with others, which showcased his best reviews. I started with the blog containing his restaurant reviews, where the awful one for Surfusion still lingered. I couldn't understand why he had attacked the restaurant in such a personal manner. He had a reputation of being fair, if a little harsh, but nothing came close to the vitriol of the review he left for Surfusion. I read it again, trying to analyse it, but the words swam before my eyes. I took a screenshot to read later, in case the police had it taken down.

When Mouse got back with the milk, we made ourselves lattes and then took the whiteboard and pens out of the office. I took a large swig of my drink without thinking and burned my tongue. Mouse laughed at me swearing and swigging down some cold milk directly from the bottle to reduce the burn. I picked up a pen and wrote out a timeline on the board, starting with Black's arrival. I plotted it out point by point as Mouse gave me the kitchen's timeline beside it.

'There's something odd about the review appearing when it did,' I said. 'I can't figure out when he posted it. I watched him writing what I imagined were comments about his food in a black notebook after he finished his starter, and again when he finished the second main course, but I never saw him use a phone.'

'He took it into the toilet with him, but I can't remember seeing it afterwards.'

'There's something strange about this whole incident.'

'Maybe he staged his death? Like some sort of macabre revenge suicide thing?'

'You've been watching too many programmes on Netflix. That's pretty far down my list of possibilities.'

Mouse pouted.

'Okay, clever clogs. What happened then?'

'I have no idea, but I think his phone may be the key. Where is it? Did he write the review before going and then schedule it to pop up when he finished eating? He had to wait for the second main course. Perhaps he mistimed it.'

'We should ask Flo if they found the phone with his body.'

'She's in bed with the flu. Donald Friske, the Brighton coroner, is on the case until she recovers. He's unlikely to tell me anything.'

'What about Joe Brennan?'

'He might tell me if I asked him, but I'd rather risk the wrath of George and save Joe for emergencies.'

'Call him. I expect he's feeling under pressure this morning. A delicious piece of cake might tempt him to be indiscreet.'

For once, George offered minimal resistance to my invitation despite being well aware of the price of my hospitality. It only took him fifteen minutes to walk from the station to Second Home. He plodded inside, large raindrops clinging to his hair, the shoulders of his suit damp, after an inclement rain shower caught him on his way to see us. Despite the constant rain we were experiencing, he refused to use an umbrella. He didn't seem to notice his damp clothes as he stood swaying in the doorway. Large bags under his eyes spoke volumes about his lack of sleep.

'Come up to the Vintage,' I said. 'There's a piece of lemon and lime drizzle with your name on it.'

'I need a coffee drip,' said George. 'I'm not sure how I'll make it through the day. I only got two hours of sleep.'

He pulled himself up the stairs by holding tight to the bannisters, puffing and panting. I felt sorry for him. He'd had some tough cases to solve recently, and his rival, DI Antrim had stolen a march on him in a couple of them. He wiped his forehead with a napkin and sniffed. I put a sweet cappuccino in front of him and cut him a decent wedge of cake. He drank half of the coffee in one go and then attacked the cake with grunts of pleasure. I waited for him to speak first, but then I noticed him gazing at our white board. Blast it. I had forgotten to put it away before he arrived. He stood up and wandered over to it, tracing the timeline with his finger. He turned to me and raised an eyebrow.

'And what may I ask is this?'

'Now, George. There's no need to get annoyed. We were only trying to help. We may have seen something you didn't.'

'And vice versa,' said Mouse.

I rolled my eyes at him and he grinned.

'You two are the bane of my life,' said George. 'But I think you're on to something here. This may help us investigate Leonard Black's motives.'

He retrieved his phone from his pocket and took a photograph.

'There's one thing we really need to know in exchange,' said Mouse.

'I don't have to tell you anything,' said George, putting his phone back in his pocket.

'Of course not. Why don't I ask you anyway and you can decide if it's a confidential piece of information or not?'

George sighed and took another bite of his cake.

'Try me,' he said.

'Did you find his mobile phone?'

George pursed his lips.

'His phone? Wait.'

He took out his notebook. We had that in common. Mouse teased me about my Poirot-like habit of writing clues in a notebook instead of on my phone, but nobody steals notebooks, and they don't have a battery that runs out. The information is safe, as long as you don't lose the actual notebook. He flipped through the pages, reading his written notes from the night before, his brow creased in concentration. Finally, he shook his head.

'No. We didn't. Forensics found a notebook, a pen, a credit card, an inhaler, but no phone.'

'So how did he post the review on his blog site?' said Mouse, arms folded.

'How indeed. We need to find the phone,' said George. 'I'll put a trace on the number.'

'Is Flo well enough to do the autopsy?' I asked.

George snorted.

'You already asked your question.'

'Come on, Dad. Be reasonable,' said Mouse.

George coloured. Mouse hardly ever called him Dad. He sighed.

'Flo is much better today. I expect she'll be in tomorrow or the next day. Donald Friske is busy in Brighton morgue, so we'll have to wait for her.'

'That's great news,' I said.

'You're not to ask her anything without running it by me first.'

'Of course not.'

Chapter 9

After George left, Mouse washed up the cups, whistling to himself, a habit he had picked up from Harry. Since he had been accepted to university, he had found it much easier to relax and enjoy simple pleasures. His relationship with George had also improved, as George had helped him get a grant from the police to study digital forensics. I didn't want to imagine how lonely I'd be without him. Me, an empty nester? Who could have predicted that?

I spent the afternoon emptying boxes of stock we had purchased from various car boot sales around Seacastle. It always surprised me how lazy people were. They would clear out their basements, or lofts, or both, into boxes, and then take them straight to a sale without checking the value of anything. A quick search on the internet could have told them they had something worth over two or three quid, but they didn't bother. I had no scruples about buying at the asking price, even if the article could be sold for ten times that much. If you're in the business, you should be interested enough to look up your articles and price them correctly.

I took the stock out of the boxes one by one and washed or wiped them to make them look their best. Mouse took each object and did an internet search on the maker's mark, working out an average price from any similar articles he found. We worked steadily and emptied two boxes before Ghita and Rohan turned up. They both looked shattered, which was hardly surprising given the circumstances. I abandoned my third box to make a large pot of tea.

'How are you both doing?' I asked, as I put the pot on the table in front of them.

'Awful,' said Ghita.

'Devastated,' said Rohan.

'How's Kieron holding up?' said Mouse.

'He's not. He's shut himself in the bedroom and refuses to come out. The police have named him a person of interest in Black's unexplained death, and he's never been so insulted.'

'That's terrible,' said Mouse, trying, and failing, to sound sincere.

Despite everything, Rohan allowed himself a smile. 'He'll get over it.'

'I'm not surprised he's sulking,' I said. 'It's such a train wreck.'

'Ah, but it's a train wreck where the driver is to blame, according to Kieron.'

'What did you do this time?' said Mouse.

'I'm the one who agreed to let Leonard Black come on opening night to review Surfusion.'

'Did he call you on your mobile?' asked Mouse.

'Yes.'

'Can you find his number?'

'I didn't think of that. Give me a second.'

Rohan flicked through the calls, and after dithering a little, he nodded.

'It's here,' he said, handing the phone to Mouse who copied the number onto his own phone.

'What are you going to do?' said Ghita.

'I'm going to call it,' said Mouse. 'I didn't want to use Rohan's number in case the person who picks up the phone recognises it and won't pick up,'

'They still might not pick up,' I said.

'Nothing ventured,' said Mouse.

We all held our breaths after he dialled.

'Hello? Am I speaking to Leonard Black?' he said.

Then he frowned and hung up.

'Nobody is answering.'

'The police need to get hold of the information on that phone,' I said. 'Can you text the number to George?'

'Done.'

'Can you hack the phone?'

'Not yet. Maybe after my first year at university.'

'Don't teach that boy to be a criminal,' said Ghita.

Rohan stroked his moustache.

'It's odd though,' he said.

'What is?' I asked.

'Leonard Black ringing me to ask for a table. As I understand it, he usually arrives incognito to eat in a restaurant, and leaves without identifying himself.'

'Now you mention it, his whole cameo was totally out of character. His clothes were Liberace-like in their flamboyance, almost like he wanted to call attention to himself,' said Ghita.

'Did you notice his wig?' I asked.

'I did. It looked like he had a guinea pig on his head,' said Rohan. 'You'd think he could afford something a little more realistic.'

'He had a full head of hair under the wig,' I said. 'I don't get it. If you want to be anonymous, why would you call attention to yourself by announcing your arrival and dressing up like that?'

'It's a mystery,' said Mouse. 'Maybe he intended to do a grand reveal. Perhaps he had a friend there who intended to film the whole thing.'

'We should check the list of attendees,' said Rohan. 'Maybe we can work out if he had an accomplice.'

'If we find out what he was doing there, perhaps we will find out why he died,' said Mouse.

'We need the results of the autopsy first, because how he died might answer that question for us. Flo will perform it over the next few days, but she may not have any immediate answers.'

'How frustrating,' said Rohan. 'What can we do meanwhile?'

'Do you remember what he ordered on the night?' I asked.

'I won't forget in a hurry. He ordered the ceviche and the Dover sole with green beans.'

'I watched him gobble down the starter and make notes in his booklet. I had the ceviche as well, so there can't have been much wrong with it,' I said.

'When he had finished the ceviche, I took his plate away and brought him the Dover sole,' said Mouse.

'He called me over after a couple of mouthfuls of fish,' said Ghita. 'He asked me if I could order him a portion of Moules Mariniere. I asked him if there was something wrong with the sole, but he wouldn't tell me. He insisted on me bringing him the second dish.'

'So, you went to the kitchen and asked Kieron for a bowl of Moules.'

'Actually, I didn't have to. He had just prepared one for me, so I took it from the counter and gave it to Leonard Black. When I came back, I asked him to make another for me and he went ballistic.'

'And then the review appeared on Leonard Black's site,' said Mouse. 'Unfortunately, my face betrayed my dismay, and Kieron insisted on reading it. He, um, he threatened to kill Black.'

'Kieron couldn't kill a wasp if it stung him ten times. There's no way he murdered Black,' said Rohan. 'Anyway, how would he have poisoned the coffee in such a short time? He was busy ranting about the review before we served the coffee.'

'So how was Black poisoned?' said Mouse.

'Who said he was poisoned?' said Ghita. 'I saw him choking. Maybe the food went down the wrong way.'

'They say the simplest explanation is often the correct one,' I said. 'But the timing of the review is too odd. I don't like coincidences when it comes to unexpected deaths.'

'The only facts we have so far are that Leonard Black died after he posted a stinking review about his dinner at Surfusion. That's our starting point. Everything else is supposition,' said Mouse.

'I think I need more tea,' said Ghita.

Chapter 10

Despite my desperation to help Rohan and Kieron clear the reputation of Surfusion, we had to wait for Flo to carry out the autopsy before we could draw any conclusions about the unexplained death of Leonard Black. I put my sleuthing aside and went to a car boot sale at Shoreham with Mouse to see if we could pick up any bargains. To my surprise, Helen asked if she could come too. She had never expressed any interest in my vintage business before, so I couldn't refuse. The three of us set out in the Mini in the cool of the early morning. The flat-calm sea sparkled under the sun. Small fishing boats were pulled up on the pebble banks with lobster pots and plastic trays piled up beside them. Seagulls perched on the prows, their black tail feathers sleek. I took the Brighton Road all along the shore until we crossed the bridge into Shoreham and headed left down the Steyning Road to the boot sale.

We pulled into the carpark just before eight o'clock and headed for the entrance to the stalls where we joined the queue. Out on the field, most of the regular sellers had already set up their wares. Some dealt out of the back of their vehicles, but most had installed temporary tables. They showcased an eclectic mix of goods ranged from second-hand clothing and toys, electrical goods in all states of repair and antiques and collectibles of all vintages. The vast majority of the articles on sale were not suitable for resale in my shop, being too new, or lacking in any distinguishing features to lure vintage collectors. However, I had my favourite dealers who always came up trumps, so I intended to head straight for the best one.

A queue of eager customers, many of them dealers like me, had already formed. Grace Wong, who sometimes bought from me instead of coming to the fair, arrived just behind us. Both the quality of her stock and the size of her prices far outstripped ours. Grace rarely came to these scrums, as they had so few articles of interest for her. Instead, she let me do the searching and then waited for me to put some new bargain in the window of Second Home she could snap up and sell for double in her shop. We greeted her with hugs, but she had a gleam in her eye, which told me all bets were off. Some of the other dealers in the queue were my direct competitors for vintage finds. I greeted the ones I knew and wondered if I could outpace them to my favourite stalls. Competition, though friendly, was also fierce. All of us needed to get in ahead of the amateurs or come away empty-handed.

The sale started, and I dashed down the middle aisle, followed by a panting Helen, arriving at my favourite stall in time to point at a gorgeous 1960s curio cupboard I knew could double as a drinks' cabinet. The dealer also had a corner cabinet with glass doors, which looked like 1970s Habitat, but I didn't recognise the model. She always loved a good banter and haggled to the last penny on her stock, but we reached a price for the pair that satisfied us both. She slapped a sold sticker on both, guaranteeing disappointment for my competition.

'Where's Mouse?' said Helen, pink in the cheeks after our mad dash.

'He's gone to the glass stall in the other aisle.'

She raised an eyebrow.

'You let him buy things for the shop? Is that wise?'

'He has great taste. And he knows what young people like. Retro's in fashion, you know.'

'But it's all so ugly. Most of this stuff could have some from Granny Vi's sitting room.'

'Some of it probably did, but fashion is always changing. A few years ago, everybody was buying Art Deco pottery. Now the prices have dropped like a stone for everything but the most exceptional pieces. That's why you have to buy what you like and not what's in vogue.'

'I'll stick to John Lewis.'

'It's a popular choice. And in fifty years it will be again, and your grandchildren will fight over your comfy chairs.'

'Come on, we'll miss the bargains.'

As I had expected, Helen's ideas on what I should buy did not coincide with mine. While I didn't mind Helen tagging along with us, I struggled to remain polite with my comments on the 'finds' she insisted on showing me. Not unlike Harry, she had zero ability to distinguish the classic from the tat and the twee. Luckily, it did not affect our haul. Mouse found a pair of Heal's pottery lamp stands and a vintage glass globe light fitting, as well as a bright yellow hand-blown glass vase. I had bought the cabinets and a couple of kitchen chairs with round backs and green vinyl seats. As the initial rush died down, dealers caught up on the gossip and drank lukewarm tea from battered flasks, which were at least as antique as most of the goods on their stalls. Helen wanted to stop and have tea at one of the refreshment stands, but I was ruthless in my dedication to the hunt for bargains and refused.

When we had finished buying, we borrowed a trolley from the dealer who sold me the cabinets and wobbled back to the car with our purchases, trying not to stop at every single stall for a browse. I saw Grace eyeing my curio cabinet from the next aisle and resolved to polish it and place it in the shop window. Mouse bought a set of classic Evelyn Waugh Penguin paperbacks for his room. He claimed they were for decoration only, but I suspected he might enjoy their anachronistic contents. Helen flopped into the front seat of the car and declared herself pooped out. I smiled to myself. Another reason to persuade Ghita to restart Fat Fighters, her exercise club. It had been an institution in Seacastle for years, but had fallen to the wayside as she fought to get the Surfusion ready for launch. I suspected we could all do with some exercise to reduce the levels of cortisol in our blood.

I drove back to town and parked as near to the shop as I could. Mouse collected the trolley from Second Home while we waited in the car. Then we took our booty to the shop. Helen demanded a coffee before we unpacked anything, so we trooped upstairs. Mouse made us all a latte while Helen devoured a piece of raspberry shortbread. Her relief showed on her face as the sugar entered her bloodstream. A family characteristic. We both had a tendency to bite if we weren't fed often enough. She played with the crumbs on her plate, a sure sign she had something to say. I could read her like a book. I waited. She pursed her lips.

'Please don't interfere in George's investigation into the death at the Surfusion. You know how cross he gets and I have to take the brunt of his moods.'

'I'm sorry George is being grumpy, but Rohan and Kieron put their savings into the restaurant. I have to help them find out what happened. George isn't always right, you know.'

'I'm aware of that, but you aren't either. Anyway, we don't know how Black died yet. It may have been a heart attack or a choking.'

She had a point. We had assumed we were dealing with a murder, but, so far, we had zero proof of that. The doorbell clanged and Ghita came up the stairs to the Vintage looking drained and on the verge of tears. All her dreams were in tatters and she was struggling to cope.

'The council has shut down the restaurant,' she said, her bottom lip wobbling. 'They are sending food hygiene inspectors to check every inch of the kitchens.'

'I'm sorry to hear that,' I said. 'But maybe that's a good thing.'

Ghita's expression changed to one of barely suppressed fury.

'How can you say that? Rohan is having a nervous breakdown and Kieron is catatonic.'

'What I meant is that public confidence needs to be restored to persuade people to eat at Surfusion. The council need to be sure they won't be poisoned by the food. Perhaps a positive hygiene inspection by them will encourage people to come back.'

'Poisoned? Who said anything about poison? That wicked man choked on his own bile.'

'You don't know that,' said Helen. 'Why don't you come and have a cup of coffee with us and calm down a little?'

I thought Ghita would explode at Helen's tone of voice. She did not like to be condescended to and Helen was an expert. Ghita ran down the stairs and tugged the door open again.

'I thought you were my friends. You don't care about the restaurant or me. I'm not staying here to be insulted.'

She stomped out into the street and down the road.

'Did I insult her?' said Helen. 'I was just trying to be nice.'

'She's overwrought. Let me deal with it,' I said. 'Stay here and help Mouse unwrap our booty.'

I skipped downstairs and followed Ghita down the street, catching up with her outside the chemist.

'Ghita, stop. Let's talk about this. We're on your side.'

'Are you? Your sister treats me like I'm a child.'

'She treats everyone like that. She's got elder sister syndrome. Come on. Let's see what Grace has got in her over-priced shop and scrounge a cup of jasmine tea.'

Chapter 11

Seeing Ghita so upset made me even more determined to find out what had happened at Surfusion that night. Black's death had shut the restaurant down before anyone got the chance to enjoy it. The internet abounded in memes and sick jokes, speculating on the course of his demise. I caught Harry and Mouse sniggering over one which featured a cartoon of George leaning over the body with a speech bubble issuing from his mouth. It said 'maybe he saw his bill'. I couldn't help smiling at the rather too accurate representation of George with his paunch poking through his shirt, but I pretended to be annoyed anyway.

'Instead of laughing at other people's misfortunes, you could try tracing Leonard Black.'

'Spoilsport,' said Harry. 'We always used to laugh at death in the army. It kept us sane.'

Sane, but not immune to damage. I didn't comment. Harry never talked about his time in the forces. He often woke during the night, shouting and sweaty, but he would never tell me what his dreams had been about. I hoped now they had reunited, that he and his brother Nick would share things they had experienced to lessen the burden, but I doubted it. He would tell me his darkest secrets one day when I least expected it.

'Despot,' said Mouse, but he typed in Leonard Black's name and started searching.

I opened my laptop and scoured the net for similar vintage finds to those we had bought at the car boot sale. I made a note of the average retail price of each one I could find so I could charge customers fair amounts for them. Harry played with Hades, dangling his favourite toy around corners and whipping it away before he could catch it. The way he giggled when Hades landed with an undignified thump on the floor warmed my heart. After a bit, Harry stood up and patted his pockets.

'Who fancies a takeaway? I'm thinking Indian.'

'Ooh, yes please,' said Mouse. 'I'll have a lamb rogan josh and poppadums.'

'And you, princess?'

'A chicken Korma with more poppadums. Do you want cash?'

'No, you're all right. I've got tons. Can I take the Mini?'

I was so absorbed in my search I hardly noticed him leave. When my phone rang, I dropped my pen on the floor with fright. George.

'Tan. It's me.'

'Hi George. What's up?'

'I thought you'd like to know. Joseph, Flo's assistant, prepped the body today for the autopsy tomorrow.'

'And?'

'It's the weirdest thing. Did you notice Black was wearing a wig?'

'Yes, we commented on that.'

'Well, that's not the only false thing about him. His goatee and moustache were glued on. He even had false padding under his clothes.'

'How old is he?'

'I don't know. About thirty, or maybe younger, it's hard to tell until Flo gets here.'

'Did he have any identifying features?'

George chuckled.

'Like a birthmark on his bum, you mean?'

'I meant tattoos.'

'There's a dragon on his right shoulder. It looks like a club mascot.'

'Or maybe he's Welsh. Can I have a photograph?'

'No, but you've got a point. That's exactly what it is. A Welsh Dragon.'

'So why did you tell me then?'

'I'm pretty sure you've got Andy, sorry, Mouse, beavering away on the computer interfering with my case. I thought it might help. You'll tell me if he finds anything.'

'Of course. Night, George.'

Mouse spun around in his chair.

'That sounds like a clue to me. Tell me what Dad said.'

'Can you wait until Harry gets back so I don't have to repeat myself?'

'Not really.'

The sound of a key in the lock saved me. Harry came in carrying the bag of takeaway curry.

'Home is the hunter. Home from the hills,' he said. 'How about a kiss to reward me for the sustenance I have provided?'

I obliged. I forgot all about Mouse until he coughed loudly.

'Would you two get a room, or even better, lay the table?'

'Oops. Sorry. Got carried away there,' said Harry.

Mouse sighed.

'I noticed. Can you please tell us what George said?'

'The body had a false goatee and moustache and fake padding under the clothes, as well as wearing a wig.'

'So, was it Black, or someone imitating him?'

'If they were imitating him, they must have known what he looks like. How else would they know how to disguise themselves?'

'They could also have been counting on nobody knowing what Black looked like and just disguised themselves on a whim,' said Harry.

'We need to trace Black's background. If we could find photographs or some sort of history for him, we can decide if the body is him, or somebody pretending to be him,' I said.

'Can we eat first?' said Mouse. 'My stomach is dissolving its own lining.'

'You poor sausage. Come and sit down.'

We soon had everything laid out on the table. The fragrant curries made my mouth water. I had a low tolerance for chilli, but all the other spices made curry irresistible to my tastebuds.

'Yum, this is fantastic,' said Mouse.

'I love curry,' said Harry. 'Nectar of the Gods.'

I took a swig of cider to calm my burning tongue and crunched up a poppadum. Harry paused with a fork halfway to his mouth, his brow furrowed.

'That cloak Black had on,' he said. 'Did it look like fancy-dress to you?'

'Now that you mention it,' said Mouse. 'It had a theatrical high collar, like Dracula would wear.'

'How many people have one of those in their wardrobe? What if he hired it?'

'You mean from a fancy dress shop?' I asked.

'Yes, or costume hire. There can't be many of them around here. Maybe we could visit them and find out who hired a cloak like that recently?'

'That's a brilliant idea. Mouse, hurry up and finish your supper. You've got lots of work to do.'

Much later that evening, Mouse stretched his arms over his head, arching his back and groaning.

'This guy doesn't exist,' he said.

'You mean you can't find him?' said Harry.

Mouse rolled his eyes.

'If I can't find him, he doesn't exist.'

'There's a body in the morgue that says he does,' I said.

'I meant Leonard Black. There's no such person. It's a pseudonym, a dead end.'

'What do we do next?'

'I found a costume hire shop in Lancing. Maybe you and Harry could go there and find out if anyone hired a cloak. I only need a name to start a search.'

'We can go tomorrow,' said Harry.

'Get some sleep, sweetheart,' I said. 'But text me the address first.'

Chapter 12

The next morning, Harry and I set out for Lancing, leaving Mouse asleep with Hades curled up on the pillow next to his head. The sun still slumbered behind a bank of clouds and the local sparrows were having a shouting competition as we walked to the car. I had uploaded the postcode to the GPS on my phone, so I followed the instructions to arrive opposite the shop, which was hard to miss. The outside had bright blue plastic cladding with the name in gold lettering. Harry tried to push the door open, but it resisted his efforts. A notice hanging on the door gave an opening time of ten o'clock.

'Breakfast?' said Harry. 'There's a greasy spoon nearby.'

'Sounds fab.'

We were soon tucking into a full English breakfast served with buttered toast and steaming mugs of strong tea. My stomach strained against the waistband of my jeans, reminding me I couldn't eat the same amount of Harry without expanding like the universe. It's so unfair. Why can men eat so much more than us without getting fat? I'd send in a complaint if it was an option. Harry patted his own tummy and beamed at me.

'I'm ready for anything now,' he said.

The owner of the shop did not arrive on time to open the shop at ten. I peered through the window and admired the rows of brightly coloured outfits lining the shop and running through the middle. I could see some rather glamorous spangled trouser suits which yelled ABBA at me. A selection of hats ranging from Napoleon Bonaparte to Pride and Prejudice teetered on narrow shelves above the rails. We had to wait another twenty minutes before he appeared puffing and panting and smoking a Rothmans which he stubbed out and dropped on the pavement. I resisted the temptation to ask him to pick it up and put it in a dustbin. He took out an enormous bunch of keys and took an age to find the correct one for the door.

'Come in, come in,' he said, with an impatience that suggested we had delayed him in some way.

As we entered, a smell of mothballs and sweat assailed me, but I tried not to grimace.

'Thank you,' I said. 'What a fabulous selection.'

'It's the best in West Sussex,' he said. 'Exceptional costumes for discerning clients. What are you looking for?'

'A cloak,' said Harry. 'It needs to be long and black with red lining.'

'Preferably with a high collar,' I said.

'That's a precise description. I have nothing like that,' said the manager. 'I've got a fabulous blue velvet one?'

'It has to be black,' said Harry. 'I've got a role as Dracula and I need to dress the part.'

The man sucked air through his teeth.

'I don't have one of those. You're out of luck.'

'Is there nowhere else we could try?' I said. 'The children will be so disappointed.'

This prompted a loud sigh of martyrdom. The owner pursed his lips.

'And why should I care about that? I've got a business to run.'

'It's for charity,' said Harry, inducing a roll of the eyes and another loud sigh.

'You could try our other shop,' he said.

'But I thought—' said Harry, quickly cut off by me.

'And where is that?' I asked.

'It's in Goring, just off the High Street.'

'Thank you. The children will be so pleased.'

His sour expression followed us out of the shop.

'Let's go straight there,' said Harry.

We didn't take long to find it. The sister shop had the same lurid colour scheme, and ABBA jumpsuits, but the manager was less refined.

'I had just the sort o' thing you wanted, but it's gorn out on hire.'

I sighed in fake exasperation at Harry.

'I told you we shouldn't leave it until the last minute,' I said.

'Don't nag, darling,' said Harry. 'I'm here now, aren't I?'

He winked at the owner who rolled his eyes in sympathy. I had never credited Harry with much skill at deception, but for a man who hated to lie, he had entered this role with consummate ease.

'When is the cloak due back in the shop?' I asked.

'Hang on a minute.'

The man took down a ledger and flipped through the pages with nicotine-stained fingers. A computer sat on his desk, presumably with a catalogue of hires in its files, but I suspected he had never bothered with it. He fumbled in a drawer and extracted a pair of reading glasses with only one lens left in them. He spat on the lens and rubbed it with his sleeve.

'That's better. Lemme see. Um, yeah, here it is.'

He pointed at an entry with his index finger. Harry and I leaned in. I placed my cleavage in his eyeline, distracting him for vital seconds while Harry had a good look at the entry.

'Wouldn't you know it? He's late getting it back here. Yer, he shoulda been in yesterday to return it. I don't know what happened.'

'Can you let us know when he brings it back?'

'Sure, just leave your number with me.'

Harry scribbled his number onto a piece of paper and handed it over. I got the distinct feeling that the owner was hoping for mine instead. The way he had fixated on my cleavage made me regret ever drawing attention to it. He seemed unable to look away. Harry took my arm and steered me out of the shop.

'Alan Miller,' he said. 'The name of the guy who hired the cloak.'

'Let's get home and ask Mouse to see if he can find a photograph of this guy. Flo can compare it to her corpse.'

'What if it's not him?'

'Then he'll know who he lent the cloak to. One way or another, we'll soon find out who died in the Surfusion. By the way, I thought you were brilliant in there, getting him to show us the ledger.'

'I think we need to thank your girlfriends.'

I laughed.

'I can't help it if he got distracted.'

'Hm. Well, I don't think we'll be going back there again.'

'Not even for the ABBA jumpsuits.'

'Especially not for those.'

Finally, we had a name we could work with. I texted it to Mouse as we headed to Second Home, my anticipation building. Harry drove with his usual deliberation, hands at ten and two on the steering wheel, just under the speed limit. Sometimes I found his military discipline infuriating, but then I remembered the times he'd defended me with the same rigour and held my tongue.

Harry dropped me off at the shop and pecked my cheek.

'See you later,' he said. 'Good luck with the sleuthing.'

For once, several customers had entered and were rummaging in the bargain baskets, squinting at the prices. I always tried to write a few words of description on the labels, but this entailed using such a small script that neither I nor my middle-aged customers could read them. A lady beckoned me over to the corner cabinet that I had purchased at the recent Shoreham car boot sale. From the way she ran her hand over the shelves, I could tell she was imagining displaying her knick-knacks on them. I gave her my best smile as I approached.

'How much is this cabinet?' she said, though I'd seen her reading the label a minute earlier.

'It's forty pounds,' I said. 'It's early Habitat. Very collectable. You have good taste.'

She smirked.

'Yes, I do. That's why I know it's overpriced and I won't pay that much for it.'

I smothered the impulse to say something rude about her ignorance. I kept my expression neutral (I think).

'And how much do you have in mind?'

'Fifteen, tops.'

I raised both eyebrows.

'Fifteen? I have a nice wicker stool I can sell to you for that price.'

She snorted and gesticulated at the stock.

'Isn't this a junk shop? Don't you know how to bargain?'

'It's the sort of shop where polite people pay less.'

She folded her arms.

'Don't you want to sell the cupboard, then?'

'Not to you.'

I heard Mouse stifle a guffaw behind me. The woman turned puce with anger or embarrassment, or both, as Mouse held the door open for her. After she had slunk away, the elderly couple who were gazing at a painting of Seacastle pier turned around and applauded.

'Oh bravo!' said the gent. 'That's how to deal with rudeness.'

'You made my day,' said his companion. 'Can you make it even better with a good price for this work of art?'

I beamed at her.

'Now, that's the way to get a reduction. You could give the other lady some lessons.'

Mouse encased the painting in bubble wrap and tied it with string to make a handle for easy carrying. The couple paid for it and left smiling and waving. I turned to Mouse who had an expression I recognised on his face; a mixture of amusement and impatience.

'You found him?'

'I think so. Do you want a coffee?'

'Yes, please. Have we got enough milk?'

Soon we were ensconced at the window table in the Vintage, sipping our coffee and examining a website Mouse had discovered called 'Prank-Your-Pals'. I found it hard to believe such a site existed, but Mouse did not seem fazed at all. The website offered the services of serial pranksters for the disruption of events or pranking a particular person. The idea did not appeal to me in the slightest, but Mouse assured me many people thought that sort of thing was funny. I remembered how much I hated Candid Camera and how popular it used to be. Horses for courses, I guessed. On the page for choosing your prankster, we found a profile for a certain Alan Miller, who claimed to be fantastic at imitation and gatecrashing. The photograph showed a handsome young man's face with a brown thatch of hair. A shiver rang down my spine as I recalled the wig falling off Leonard Black's head to reveal an identical covering.

'Who runs the site?' I asked.

'I'm not sure. I can find out. Do you think it's him?'

'I don't know. It seems likely. Can you copy the photograph and send it to George? Flo should do the autopsy today. It will help her identify him.'

Minutes after Mouse sent him the photograph, George rang my cell phone.

'Tan? Hi. Thanks for the photograph. Flo is pretty sure the body on her slab belongs to Alan Miller. We'll ask his relatives to come down to the station to identify him.'

'How terrible for them! Have they already been informed?'

'Once we get confirmation of who is his next of kin, I will send Joe Brennan with the new family liaison officer to inform them of Miller's death. Joe will play it by ear from there.'

'What a horrible tragedy. I won't ask you about the autopsy, but can you please tell me one thing?'

'Maybe.'

'Did you find a mobile phone at the scene?'

'Not yet, but I sent the boys back in to look again.'

'How did he send the review to Leonard Black's blog?'

George didn't reply. I waited. He cleared his throat.

'I don't know.'

'I can't remember seeing him use a phone. I watched him write comments in a black notebook.'

'Yes, I saw him scribbling in it. But we have examined the notebook, and he had not reviewed his meal in there, just made a series of meaningless doodles.

The notebook seems to have been a prop. Didn't he go to the toilet at one stage?'

'Perhaps he sent the review from there?'

'I'll have them check there again for a phone. But if not, maybe Alan Miller had nothing to do with the review. We'll follow up Prank Your Pals and find out who hired Alan Miller.'

'Could he have been murdered because of the review?'

'We don't know he was murdered. He seems to have choked. He had an EpiPen in his cloak, so it is likely he suffered from a serious allergy. Flo is going to send the contents of his stomach to the lab to check on the contents. We should have the results in a week or two. I put a rush on it, but everyone does, so I doubt we can get them quicker.'

'Two steps forward, one step back?'

'Something like that. At least we've identified the body, thanks to you and Mouse.'

'But if the body is Alan Miller, where is Leonard Black, and who uploaded the review?'

'All good questions. None with an answer yet.'

Chapter 13

George tasked his technical team with searching the restaurant again while I waited for the findings from the autopsy. The sunny weather had enticed an increased number of day trippers to Seacastle, and Second Home benefited from their custom. The Vintage had a steady stream of extra clients enjoying a coffee and a slice of cake, as well as browsing the shop and purchasing items which appealed to them. I took advantage of the increased footfall to sell smaller items which had been languishing in boxes at the back of the shop for months. Mouse co-opted Leanne, who had been shocked to the core by the death at Surfusion, to help him at the Vintage by waiting on tables and washing the crockery. She appreciated the money with the restaurant closed and she soon recovered her humour a little. I grew accustomed to hearing her chirpy banter upstairs, as I kept the cash register ringing downstairs.

Among the clientele one day, I noticed a woman staring up at the vintage glass fishing floats handing from the ceiling in rope netting. The sunlight made the glass throw a coloured glow about the shop like a low-key disco.

'Are those for sale then?' she asked, her tone sharp.

Her question pierced the momentary lull in the conversation upstairs. I heard Leanne drop a teaspoon in the kitchenette.

'Yes, everything's for sale, except the staff and the coffee machine,' I said.

She did not respond to my humour.

'Can you get them down for me?' she said.

'Certainly. Which colours would you like to see?'

'That blue one, and the aquamarine, and the green one.'

'One moment, please.'

I shouted up the stairs to Mouse.

'Could you please fetch the stepladder for me? We need to take down some of these fishing floats.'

'Mouse? What sort of name is that?' she muttered, gazing out of the shop door. She appeared to be looking at the Surfusion. 'The new restaurant is still shut down then?'

'They're waiting for the Council's food hygiene team to complete their inspections and give them the all clear to open again.'

'Serves them right for using Ed Murray to supply them. This wouldn't have happened if they had used my husband in the first place.'

I thanked my lucky stars Roz had not come in to help me. I could only imagine her reaction to that comment.

'Is your husband a fisherman?' I asked.

'Yes. Keith Matling. He sails out of Shoreham.' She moistened her lips with her tongue. 'I heard the dead man died of an allergy. Dreadful for his family. Do you think they'll close it down for good?'

'I don't know. I hope not. The owners are friends of mine.'

'Far be it from me to criticise, but I think you need new friends. They're as camp as Christmas, those two.'

Mouse, who had climbed the ladder and waited for instructions, made a face at me. I gesticulated at the floats.

'The floats are twenty pounds each. Can you tell my son which ones you would like?'

'Twenty quid? I need them to decorate our fishmongers, not a ballroom. What about ten?'

'I can't reduce the price. I need to make a profit. Would you like Mouse to pass you down one or not?'

'I've changed my mind.'

Mouse came down the ladder with deliberation and folded it up without taking his eyes off her. She tutted and left the shop muttering 'daylight robbery' just loud enough for us to hear.

'Another satisfied customer,' said Mouse.

'We're having a run of bad luck. If the husband is half as aggressive as his missus, it's no wonder Ed's keeping a low profile.'

Mouse took the ladder to hide it away at the back of the shop and I served a customer who had found a rather nice lampshade in one of my rummage baskets. As usual, I had forgotten to price it. She clung to it like a child with their teddy bear.

'It's perfect,' she whispered. 'I can't believe it. I've searched for months to find this colour.'

'It's expensive, I'm afraid,' I said.

Her pretty eyes almost popped out of her head with anxiety.

'Oh dear. How much is it?'

'Four pounds fifty.'

'Oh! I see. You're only joking.'

She fished a fiver out of her embroidered handbag and handed it over, quivering with excitement. She left without relinquishing her grip on the shade. I didn't bother to offer her a bag for it. My cell phone sounded under the counter as I watched her leave with her prize. Flo's name appeared on the screen and my heart rate quickened.

'Any chance of a coffee?' said the message.

Luckily, the flow of clients had stopped by the time she arrived at Second Home. I sent Mouse away with Leanne. They both sulked at being ejected. He loved Flo, but I needed privacy for our talk, and I didn't want Leanne to feel left out by asking only her to go home. Flo turned up in a pair of purple hareem pants and a bright pink blouse, her signature untidy bun having all but escaped from its binding.

'I'm dying of thirst,' she said. 'The Gobi Desert has more options than the police station. I can't face another instant coffee with skimmed milk.'

'How about a glass of fresh lemonade? Mouse made it for the lunchtime rush, but we have a spare glass or two in the fridge.'

'Yes, please. But where is Mouse? I had hoped to see him and give him a squeeze.'

'I needed to get rid of his friend.'

'Girlfriend?'

'Not yet. Still exploring that option, I think.'

'I'm jealous. Mouse is mine.'

'And shall remain so. What news of Alan Miller?'

'He died of anaphylactic shock.'

'But didn't George inject him with an EpiPen?'

'He did, but unfortunately Alan Miller had asthma and that exacerbates the allergic reaction and increases the likelihood of a fatality.'

'How unfortunate. Was he allergic to shellfish?'

'I'm not sure what caused the reaction yet. The stomach's contents are on their way to the forensics lab for testing.'

'So, it might not be an allergy to shellfish that killed him?'

'All options are open at this point. We've sent samples from all the dishes that were served on the night. Unfortunately, we don't have his plates. Leanne washed them by mistake on the night. I thought George might murder her too.'

'You think Miller may have been murdered?'

'Not really. Anything's possible, but it seems unlikely. George told me the guy worked as a professional prankster. Why murder him? It's looking like a case of misadventure.'

'That doesn't explain what he was doing there.'

'There's nothing to stop you from finding out.'

After Flo left, I cashed up and got ready to go home. It didn't take me long. Even on busy days, the vast majority of people tapped their cards on the reader, which resulted in less temptation for burglars and shoplifters. All I had to do was print out a roll of the transactions and a total and check it against the ledger.

I had washed the last cups and wiped down the tables when I heard the doorbell clang. I wondered if Mouse had forgotten something, but I thought it unlikely. He never parted from his laptop bag. His whole life was contained within it. I came downstairs to find Kieron hovering in the doorway. He had never come to Second Home without Rohan before. I could count on the fingers of one hand the times he had come at all. His face loomed unnaturally pale in the half light.

'Hi Kieron. This is an honour. Can I offer you a sixties lava lamp or a set of faux Clarice Cliff bookends?'

He didn't smile.

'I thought I saw Dr Barrington leave the shop just now.'

For a few seconds, I couldn't imagine who that might be. Then I remembered. Flo of course. I rearranged my features.

'Yes, you did. She came in for a cup of coffee and a chat. Did you want to speak to her about something?'

He shook his head.

'Did she, did she tell you anything about, you know?'

A bead of sweat glistened on his brow.

'About what?'

'Leonard Black dying at the Surfusion. What happened to him?'

I had forgotten that the real identity of the deceased was not common knowledge outside George's circle. I wondered if it would be correct to mention that yet. The death could have resulted from misadventure, but what if someone had meant to murder Leonard Black? Someone like Kieron, in a blind rage after reading the review on Black's blog. I stalled.

'She sent contents of the stomach for testing, so we won't know the results for a while.'

He wavered and grabbed the counter. I thought he might collapse.

'Is there something you should tell me?' I asked.

'Why would I do that? We all know you blab to George,' he said.

He stumbled back outside again, leaving me opened-mouthed. What did he know about the death that he couldn't tell me?

Chapter 14

I arrived home worn out from my encounters at Second Home, desperate for the reassurance of my family. The Grotty Hovel beckoned me into its warm interior and wrapped its walls around me in a comforting embrace. The enticing aroma of a roast chicken permeated my sinuses and made me salivate. My low mood had been caused by hunger. I sunk into an armchair and tried to enjoy the anticipation of a delicious supper. I wasn't the only one. Hades had parked himself at the entrance to the kitchen, waiting for tasty treats to come his way. Harry emerged, drying his hands on a dishcloth.

'Are you okay?' he said, coming over to kiss me on the top of my head. 'You looked exhausted.'

'Mostly hungry, but today was heavy-duty on the emotional front too.'

'What did Flo say?' said Mouse, popping his head out of the kitchen.

'Miller died of anaphylactic shock. She thinks it might be an accident.'

'Might?' said Harry. 'So it could be deliberate?'

'Theoretically. They'll need to complete the analysis of the samples from the kitchen first.'

'Why would anyone kill a prankster? It makes little sense,' said Mouse.

'It does if they thought he was the real Leonard Black. There must have been many people who resented his ability to make or break a restaurant. How well do we know Rohan and Kieron, anyway? They worked for months to get the Surfusion off the ground. Months of sacrifice and expenditure disappeared in an instant when that review got published. I've seen men kill for less,' said Harry.

'But that's in the army, sweetheart. Would civilians murder a man because of a review?'

'Kieron is capable of anything when he loses his temper,' said Mouse. 'I've seen him in action, and it's not pretty. He screamed at Ghita and accused her of killing the critic with her biscuits. I pointed out that she had made them in the Surfusion kitchen, so anyone could have poisoned them.'

'Poisoned them? Didn't Flo call it an accident?'

'Who said the biscuits were poisoned?' I said, dizzy with hunger and totally confused by this new theory.

Hades yowled loudly to draw attention to his impatient wait for chicken, and the likelihood of him expiring from hunger in the near future. Harry laughed.

'We'd better talk about this after we've eaten, or Hades might take a bite out of us soon.'

'Can you carve, please?' I said. 'And give that maggot the gizzards from the gravy to chew. That'll keep him quiet for a while.'

'I threw them out,' said Mouse. 'I didn't realise you used them to make the gravy.'

'There's chicken Bisto in the cupboard. Give Hades some soggy skin instead. He can have meat when we've finished eating.'

Harry and Mouse had produced a feast worthy of the finest restaurant. I gorged myself on roast potatoes. There's nothing better than a roast dinner for restoring your humour and expanding your waistline. Harry took the plates out to the kitchen and gave Hades some scraps of chicken meat. We all took our glasses of wine to the sofa and I undid the top button of my trousers.

'The dryer is definitely shrinking my clothes,' I said. 'Where were we on the Surfusion mystery?'

'We were talking about Flo's autopsy. How long will it take to get the results from the forensic lab?' said Harry.

'It could take weeks,' I said. 'That laboratory is always backed up.'

'But what about Surfusion?' said Mouse. 'Even if the council let them open it again, nobody will come.'

'They might do if we can get the real Leonard Black to retract the review and issue a new one,' said Harry.

'What if the death of the prankster is only a horrible coincidence, and nothing to do with the other events of that evening? If we ignore it for a moment, we are left with two attempts to destroy the reputation of Surfusion; the vitriolic review, and the prankster. We can presume somebody sent him to cause a scene. He just didn't get the chance to act it out, at least not the one he had planned.'

'Somebody really wants to destroy the Surfusion, and they are prepared to do almost anything to achieve it,' said Mouse.

'We can't let them get away with it. George doesn't want us interfering with the inquiry into Miller's death, but that doesn't stop us from investigating the incidents on opening night. Someone hired that prankster and probably also hacked Leonard Black's account to leave the review.'

'We need to find those saboteurs,' said Harry. 'Who would want to do this?'

'I've got some ideas,' I said.

'Let me put up the whiteboard,' said Mouse.

'We don't have one.'

'Metaphorical. I'll take notes on my phone and send them to you both.'

'A list of suspects would be handy,' said Harry.

'People with personal grudges against Rohan and Kieron should be top of the list,' said Mouse.

'Didn't you tell me Rohan's brother is threatening to tell their parents about him being gay?' said Harry. 'Maybe he's trying to break up the relationship by bankrupting them.'

'That's a good call,' said Mouse, tapping on his keyboard.

'What about Kieron's ex-boyfriend? He got dumped for Rohan. Maybe this is his revenge,' I said.

'Isn't it a little extreme?' said Harry.

'Hell hath no fury,' said Mouse.

'Who else could want to close it down?' said Harry. 'What about a local restaurant? Is there one that specialises in seafood? The owners might have sabotaged Surfusion to prevent new competition from stealing their clients.'

'We can certainly research that,' I said. 'Put it on the list.'

We sat in silence for a moment. Hades sat on the lid of his laundry basket and gave himself a bath with his tongue. Harry had cut an opening in the side to give Hades easy access, so now he used the lid as his vantage point on the world. I looked up to the ceiling for inspiration in the cracked paint and a vintage fisherman's float caught my eye.

'What about the fisherman?' I asked.

'Which fisherman?' said Harry.

'When Mouse and I were in the shop today, we had a horrible client who claimed to be the wife of a fisherman who tried to supply the restaurant with his catch.'

'And she said something about it being the owner's fault the restaurant got closed down because they chose Ed Murray instead of her husband,' said Mouse.

'What was her name?' said Harry.

'I don't remember. She said he sailed out of Shoreham.'

'She wanted to look at the vintage floats to buy them for their fishmongers,' said Mouse.

'You're right. There can't be that many fishmongers in Shoreham. We could easily find her again if we wanted to.'

'Do you want to drive over with me tomorrow morning and have a look?' said Harry. 'I'm not busy.'

'That would be great. Can you open up the shop Mouse? Roz is coming to help us tomorrow, so you won't be alone.'

'Okay. I'll research some of these suspects too. Do you know the names of Rohan's brother or Kieron's boyfriend?'

'No, but I suspect Ghita does. She is due to deliver a cake tomorrow. I'm not sure she will actually bake one. But you can get the names from her.'

Chapter 15

Harry and I set out to Shoreham in my Mini on a bright, windy morning, leaving Mouse to open the shop with Roz. We lowered the windows and let the fresh sea air blow away the cobwebs. The small fishing skiffs were pulled up onto the pebble banks loaded with lobster pots and nets ready to go back out to sea. Some juvenile seagulls lurked beside them, pecking at the pebbles in the vain hope of finding scraps from the last haul. It reminded me of the first time I saw Herbert and I crossed my fingers he was doing okay without a supply of bacon rinds and toast.

Our van made rapid progress through the light traffic and we soon arrived at Shoreham wharf, turning into the car park which overlooked the channel between the wharf and the spit. The fishing boats pulled up to the wharf were riding high in the water having already disgorged their night's catches onto the wharf. Opposite the wharf, new blocks of flats occupied the spit with views out on the beach and English Channel. A strong breeze whipped my hair into the air and I struggled to tie it into a bun. I caught Harry gazing at me and read his expression. I wrinkled my nose at him.

'I'm bewitched,' he said. 'Did that lot at the coven teach you any spells?'

'Hopefully I can remember one for enticing information out of unwilling interviewees.'

'I have a feeling you might need black magic for that.'

We entered the fishmonger through a gateway composed of two giant, painted lobsters. I found them mildly sinister, but Harry stroked their claws 'for good luck'. The gleaming interior of the shop smelled of fish and ozone. A chrome counter showcased a stunning display of myriad species of crustacean and flat fish, slabs of cod and haddock alongside fresh herring, trout and whiting. Their bright skins shone amongst the ice cubes, advertising their freshness. Bream, turbot, Dover sole, and monkfish jostled for position amid plaice and salmon fillets. Dishes of mussels and scallops were separated by regimented lines of king prawns and lobsters with their claws held shut with elastic bands.

'Wow! Why do I feel hungry suddenly?' said Harry.

'It's the best selection on the south coast,' said a voice. 'Nobody beats us on price or quality.'

A burly man stepped out of a back office; his arms covered in tattoos. 'What can I get you folks today? The turbot is fresh off the boat this morning.'

'I'm looking for a fisherman,' I said. 'Isn't your friend up to the job then?' he said, eyeing Harry's arms.

Harry's bonhomie evaporated, and he gave the man a hard stare.

'No insult intended, mate,' said the man. 'Any particular one?'

'Um, I can't remember his name, but I know he sails out of Shoreham.'

'I'll need more than that to identify him.'

'He owns a fishmonger in town.'

'Which town is that then? We're the only one in Shoreham.'

'Oh. I see.'

But I didn't. Was this the man we were looking for? Perhaps my difficult customer lied to me. She obviously had no intention of buying any floats that day.

'What if I described his wife?'

He raised an eyebrow.

'I don't know what you're insinuating, but I'm not sure I like where you're going with this.'

'She came into my shop and inquired about the fisherman's floats we have for sale. She was asking about the death at the Surfusion Restaurant.'

The man stiffened.

'Are you the lady who owns a vintage shop on Seacastle High Street?'

'That's right,' I said.

He frowned and crossed his arms.

'I'd like you to leave right now.'

'Please. I need his name. I just want to ask him some questions.'

'Forget it. You've come to the wrong place. I can't help you.'

'That's okay, mate,' said Harry. 'I don't suppose you'd like to sell us some plaice fillets while we're here?'

'No. I wouldn't.'

There was no point arguing. His metaphorical shutters had come down.

'That's him, isn't it?' I asked as we walked back to the car. 'What a wasted trip.'

'I think so, but it wasn't a total washout.'

He handed me a business card.

'Keith Matling! That rings a bell. It's him alright. We should give the name to Mouse and see what he comes up with.'

'Let's go before he sends us to find Davy Jones's locker.'

After texting the name to Mouse, we drove back to Seacastle. We were met by Roz, whose eyes were shining with malice, a sure sign she had some juicy gossip to tell me.

'I can't believe you went to see the battling Matlings without me.'

'You know them?' said Harry.

'Doesn't everyone?'

'Roz knows everybody,' I said.

'Of course I do. They're notorious in our circle. When they're not fighting each other, they pick a fight with someone else. It's rumoured that he's got a dodgy past, but people are jealous of his success with the fishmongers, so...'

'How did Ed persuade Kieron to use him as a supplier?'

'The Matlings prefer large orders. Kieron didn't want to use frozen fish at Surfusion, and Ed was happy to provide smaller amounts more often. If he doesn't have what Kieron wants, he will source it from his friends' catch. Personal service wins the day every time.'

'Has Ed spoken to George yet?'

'About what?'

As much as I love Roz, giving her inside information on a case is like broadcasting it from the rooftops with a megaphone. I hedged.

'I guess they'll be tracing all the food served on the night. After all, he died at a restaurant.'

'Ed only sells fresh produce. It wasn't anything to do with him.'

'Nobody said it was. They have to cover all bases.'

'I thought the victim had a heart attack.'

'He probably did, but they still have to check.'

'What does Flo say?'

'I don't think she had the results back from the lab yet,' I said, crossing my fingers behind my back.

'You'll let me know when you do?'

'Of course.'

Chapter 16

The next morning, Harry and I drove up to London to deliver a load of furniture to his cousin Tommy's warehouse in the east end of London. We set out bright and early, leaving Mouse to run the shop with Roz. Leanne had cried off again, claiming to have a cold, but she had been behaving strangely. I wondered if she had had a tiff with Mouse. No doubt I would find out eventually. I had the address of the Prank-Your-Pals in my phone. We planned to drop in there after delivering the furniture to see if we could find out who hired Alan Miller. On our way to London, we drove into a bank of torrential rain. Despite running the windscreen wipers at full speed, it became almost impossible to see where we were going. The traffic slowed to a crawl, and Harry sighed.

'I could really do with some Led Zeppelin to cheer me up.'

'Me too. I miss the old van. This is more comfortable, but it doesn't feel right without music.'

'Has Mouse put an app on your phone yet?'

'He has, but I don't want to pay for music I already own.'

'Shall I sing?'

'Maybe not.'

We amused ourselves by counting red cars and betting on the drips running down my side window pane.

I hadn't told Harry about my search for a cassette player. It hadn't been successful yet, but I hadn't given up yet.

Tommy came out of his office when we pulled up outside the warehouse. He had abandoned his customary old, green woollen sweater for a bright acrylic, faux Argyll patterned one. His eyes opened wide when he saw the van.

'And I thought I had pushed the boat out with my new sweater,' he said. 'That's a smart van you've got there. It must have cost a pretty penny. What happened to Uncle Bill's van?'

'It's a long story,' said Harry. 'It is nice to have a van that's a little more reliable. Unfortunately, it hasn't got music yet. We are missing our tapes.'

'And what's stopping you from taking the cassette deck out of the old van?' he said.

We both looked at each other.

'But it got sent for scrap,' I said. 'It's too late.'

'Honestly. You must be made of money,' said Tommy. 'What have you got for me today, then?'

I left them to banter while they emptied the van. I knew from experience there was no point offering to help. Tommy prided himself on his strength and competed with Harry to lift the most.

Once they had finished unloading the van, we had an enormous, tasty sausage sandwich each for lunch at the local café and then set out for Prank-Your-Pals. The office was on the top floor of a run-down building in a back street in Bermondsey. Harry buzzed the intercom, and the door opened with a creak of protest. The ancient carpet petered out on the second floor of the shabby staircase and we laboured up the bare stairs to the top floor, panting with effort after our lunch. The door of Prank-Your-Pals opened to reveal a tiny office with two desks separated by a plywood partition. The young woman who opened the door smiled a welcome.

'We don't get many clients at the office,' she said. 'It makes a pleasant change.'

'What do you want?' said the man behind the other desk.

'We're here about a prank you carried out last week,' said Harry.

The man rolled his eyes.

'We don't accept any responsibility for pranks. You need to get a sense of humour.'

'What about pranks which kill somebody?'

The man's plump cheeks imploded.

'Killed someone? But it's not possible. We won't accept bookings for anything dangerous.'

'Do you have a man called Alan Miller on your books?' I asked.

'Alan Miller. Yes, we did, but I fired him.'

'Fired? Why?'

'Not that it's any of your business, but he left me in the lurch. He didn't turn up for a job last week.'

'That would have been difficult, seeing as he was dead,' I said.

The woman stifled a gasp with her hand.

'Dead? But how?' she said.

'We're not sure yet,' I said. 'He died on the job at Seacastle.'

'But we hadn't booked a prank for Seacastle, had we, Michelle?'

'No, boss. I'd know if we had. There's nothing in the diary.'

'Could he have gone off the book?' said Harry.

'I suppose so, but I'd have fired him for that too.'

'Is there anyone who might know how he ended up in Seacastle?'

'Do I look like his mother?' said the man. 'Thanks for letting me know about him, but we're busy, so I'd like you to leave.'

They were so busy they practically had cobwebs strung between them, but we left anyway. As we descended the stairs, the young woman ran after us, her feet clattering on the wood, and thrust a piece of paper into my hand.

'He was a nice man,' she said. 'He had a fiancée who loved him. If anyone knows who hired him, she will.'

A tear ran down her cheek and she brushed it away before going back upstairs. I wondered if she had had a crush on him. I sometimes forgot dead bodies had families and history in the thrill of the chase. I chastised myself for not noticing her distress earlier.

When we got outside, I dialled the number on the piece of paper. At first, no one answered, and I was about to hang up when a sad whisper broke the silence.

'Hello?'

'Hi. My name is Tanya Bowe. I'm from Seacastle and I would love to talk to you if you can spare me a few minutes.'

'Seacastle? But that's where Alan died. Are you press?'

'No. I'm a friend of the owners of Surfusion where Alan—'

'Do you know anything about what happened to him?'

'We were at the restaurant. We saw everything. Do you mind if we come and see you?'

'Not at all. I'm in Clapham. I'll text my address to you.'

'We'll be there shortly. I'm with my partner, Harry Fletcher, in Bermondsey now. Is it okay if he comes too?'

'I'm in no fit state to receive visitors, but I don't mind if you don't. Can you please buy a pint of milk on your way here? I haven't been out for days.'

'Of course. Would you like anything else?'

'No thanks. I haven't been eating much.'

Susanne Jones lived in a tiny flat on the lower ground floor of a subdivided Victorian terraced house. She came to the door wrapped in a ragged terry dressing gown, her cheeks red and blotchy with crying. Her ravaged face spoke volumes about the misery Alan's untimely death had caused her. I didn't know whether to shake her hand or hug her.

'I'm so sorry for your loss. I'm Tanya and this is my partner, Harry.'

Harry shuffled in behind me, unable to articulate his feelings. Too late, I remembered the loss of his beloved wife, Cathy. If anyone knew how Susanne felt, it was him. She showed us into the sitting room where we sat on the sofa opposite a table covered in dirty cups and empty crisp packets. She gestured at the mess.

'Sorry about this. I've not felt like cleaning recently.'

'Don't be. I lost my wife a few years ago. They had to dig me out of my house after a few months. Would you like me to make us a pot of tea?'

She started to get up, but Harry shook his head.

'I'll do it. We brought milk,' he said, collecting the dirty cups and rubbish as if it were the most natural thing in the world.

Susanne wavered.

'Leave him to it,' I said. 'He's ex-army; good in a crisis and excellent at foraging in foreign terrains. How are you holding up?'

'I'm not. I can't get any information from the police about what happened to Alan, just that his death is unexplained so far. Were you really there on the night?'

'Yes, we were. Actually, we were sitting at the table next door to him. He had called ahead, pretending to be a famous food critic, so he got first class service from the owners. He seemed to have an enjoyable time until—'

'Did he suffer?'

'I don't think so. He just keeled over. The forensic consultant thinks it may have been anaphylactic shock. Was Alan allergic to anything?'

'Peanuts. He couldn't go anywhere near them. He always carried an EpiPen just in case.'

'What about seafood?'

'Not as far as I know. We used to eat Sushi as a treat sometimes.'

'Can you tell me why he went to the Surfusion that night?'

'He got a phone call from someone asking if he would prank the restaurant. The caller offered him three times the usual rate. We were saving up for the wedding, you know, so he couldn't refuse. Prank-Your-Pals didn't pay much and sometimes the work would dry up.'

'Do you know who hired him?'

'I'm sorry. I don't know. The man paid in cash up front. I didn't see him, but he had a dark blue car, or maybe black. I don't know which make of car, as I can't tell one from the other, but it had a sticker in the back window.'

'Was it an estate car? With a square back?'

'No, a normal one, like an upside-down soup plate.'

A saloon car, like George's. That might help.

'How did Alan get to Seacastle?'

'He went by train. We don't have a car. The man who hired him said he would pick him up at the railway station.'

Harry bustled in with a tray containing a teapot and cups, a milk jug and a pile of hot buttered toast. He poured us all a cup and put the plate of buttered toast and honey in front of Susanne. She put her hand up to refuse, but then the smell penetrated her fug of sadness. She reached over and took a piece, wolfing it down in three bites, quickly followed by a second. Harry smiled, and then he winked at me. I let her attack the toast, sipping my tea and enjoying the quiet moment. When she had finished the toast, she gulped down her tea. She looked up startled, when I coughed to attract her attention.

'Oh my goodness. What a pig I am! I didn't offer you any. It was so delicious.'

'We ate a sausage sandwich for lunch,' said Harry. 'I'm glad you enjoyed it.'

She wiped her mouth to clean the butter from her lips.

'Why are you doing this?' she said. 'What's Alan to you? Did you know him?'

'The owners of the restaurant are friends of ours. He went to their opening night. They put all their savings into Surfusion, and now it has been shut down as a precaution by the council. We are determined to find out what really happened to Alan, so they can reopen it.'

Her eyes opened wide.

'You think it wasn't an accident?'

'I didn't say that, but we have to follow all the leads no matter where they take us. Alan's death may have been collateral damage, or just a horrible coincidence. We don't know yet.'

'Will you keep me informed?'

'Of course. We also share our findings with the police so if we can help them get to the root of the mystery we will.'

We left soon afterwards, as Susanne looked as if she needed a long sleep, perhaps her first since the murder. As we were driving home, Harry cleared his throat, a sure sign he had something to say.

'I have a confession to make,' he said.

'You got help making the toast?'

He laughed.

'No, not that. It's about my old van.'

'I'm listening.'

'It's sitting outside my house. I couldn't face taking it to the scrap yard right away, so I've been working my way up to it.'

'You mean you still have the tape deck?'

'Yup. It's right there in the dashboard. I had completely forgotten about it being there.'

'Let's remove it. Then we can share the latest news with Mouse.'

'And George.'

'Okay. Him too.'

Chapter 17

I could tell from the way George strode into the Grotty Hovel that I wasn't the only one with new ideas about Alan Miller's death. Helen followed him in, beaming to see everybody. Hades rushed up to her and wound himself around her legs, purring like a train. She leaned down to stroke him and he glanced in my direction, ready to gloat. I knew that trick already and pretended not to notice. He stuck his tail in the air and stalked past me to the cat flap, jumping through in one bound and disappearing into the brambles.

Harry offered them a drink before supper. George asked for a glass of red wine, but Helen refused a drink. When I raised an eyebrow at her, she made signs of turning a steering wheel. She was a stickler for drink driving rules, so this made sense. Despite being a police officer, George sometimes played with the limits. Like many men his age, he considered himself an even better driver after a couple of glasses of wine, ignoring the statistics and the law in the process. I had given up trying to convince him otherwise, and I could see that Helen had also failed. I made her a jug of elderflower cordial and joined her in a glass so she didn't feel left out. George insisted on clinking everyone's glass in celebration.

'You've cracked the case then?' I asked, knowing the answer.

'I'm getting close. There are a few loose ends to tie up here and there.'

'George is so clever,' said Helen. 'I don't know how he does it.'

She squeezed his arm and his chest lifted and stuck out, creating the illusion that he had a hidden valve in his arm muscle.

'Good old-fashioned police work wins the day every time,' he said, glowing under her praise.

'Are you going to let us in on it?' said Harry. 'You know we won't go around telling people whodunnit.'

George rolled his eyes at this request, but his smug face told me he couldn't resist showing off to us. He took a slug of wine.

'After the first abortive search for evidence, I decided we should go over the place with a fine-toothed comb. The team completed a finger-tip search in every nook and cranny of the restaurant. We got lucky and one of them found a mobile phone hidden behind the shutter in the men's toilet.'

'That's fantastic,' I said.

Naturally, he had not acknowledged it as being my idea in the first place. I sighed inwardly.

'Anyway, our techies have analysed the call logs and social media apps for us. This phone was not used to post the nasty review on Leonard Black's blog. It seems to be a coincidence that Miller went to the toilet shortly before the review turned up on the blog that night. We only know Miller called Rohan from the same phone to make the booking for Surfusion, but I think we're close to the truth of this story.'

I could see holes in this theory, but I forced myself to refrain from saying anything. Mouse did not feel constrained to a polite congratulation.

'Who was the mobile registered to?' he asked.

'The phone? Um, it was a burner phone, so nobody.'

'How do you know it was Miller's then?' said Harry.

'We don't. Yet. But we're working on it. The technicians found a partial fingerprint on the chip, which they are working to identify.'

'Does it belong to Miller?' said Mouse.

'No. But it may have been inserted by a random shop assistant. The phone could still have belonged to Miller.'

George tapped his fingers on the table and fixed Mouse with a steely glare.

'Can I ask why there is a call from your number on Miller's phone?'

Mouse avoided his eyes.

'Rohan gave me the number of the person who called to reserve a table in Black's name. I called it to see if anyone would answer.'

'Before you told me about it? No, don't bother replying. I should have known.'

Mouse shrugged. I could resist no longer.

'But why did Miller target the restaurant? What motive did he have?' I asked.

'We don't know that yet either. That's one of the loose ends we're investigating.'

'How did he die? Did someone plan to kill him, or was his death a coincidence?' said Helen.

George's ears turned red. He hated coincidences. His bubble of confidence deflated as we cross-questioned him.

'And why didn't his EpiPen work?' asked Harry. 'Is that a coincidence too?'

'We haven't had the lab reports yet,' said George, fidgeting. 'I'm sure it will be resolved soon enough. I'm really not allowed to answer most of these questions.'

Helen nodded, but her brow had creased. George had turned a frustrated shade of purple. I took pity on him.

'I don't know if this is any help, but Harry and I visited the Prank-Your-Pals office today,' I said. 'They assured us they didn't send Miller on assignment to Surfusion.'

'But what was he doing there if they didn't send him?' said Helen.

'Somebody contacted him without going through the company. He went as a private hire.'

'Did they tell you that?' said George.

'No, his girlfriend did. We met her too.'

George gave an exasperated sigh.

'Honestly, Tan. You're trying my patience here. I asked you not to interfere with the investigation.'

'But we haven't. We're trying to find out why someone is attempting to sabotage the Surfusion. Rohan and Kieron are friends of ours, and their livelihood is being threatened by this horrible incident on their opening night. Miller's death may be an accident, but the sabotage is intentional.'

George took a swig of his wine. He rubbed his chin.

'But if Miller was an unwitting participant in the sabotage, how come he's dead now?'

'Maybe somebody wanted to clear up the loose ends?' I said.

'I know you don't want to consider this possibility, but maybe the owners killed him thinking he had sabotaged Surfusion,' said George. 'A personal vendetta can go both ways. You were there on the night, Andy. Are you sure you heard nothing that might give me a lead?'

Mouse shrugged. He hated being called Andy. George had forgotten again and reduced his chance of penetrating Mouse's resistance to tattle on his pals. Then he coloured. I knew he had remembered Kieron's fury at the review. George noticed too.

'You should tell me if you have any suspicions. Innocent people don't get sent to prison on my watch, but we need to follow any leads, no matter how tenuous.'

He had switched to police jargon now. Mouse frowned.

'But I told you already. I showed Kieron the review after he sent out the second main course to Miller. How could he have known about Miller's allergy?'

'What about putting something in the coffee? Or the biscuits? We don't know there wasn't poison used too.'

'Anyone of us could have put something in the coffee, or the biscuits,' said Mouse. 'That includes me.'

'You mean anyone in the kitchen at the time?'

'Of course. Who else?'

'We need to do some more checking. We'll soon know how he died. Flo's expecting the results on the stomach contents any day now. We've also sent samples of all the foods and drinks from the kitchen to check for contamination. If Miller was killed because of the review, this will become a murder inquiry.'

'But it still doesn't tell us why somebody is trying to shut the Surfusion,' I said. 'And that's what we were investigating.'

'There's no need to go around in circles,' said George. 'I've got the general gist. We'll put out an announcement about the real identity of the body in the next day or two.'

'Can we keep looking?' I asked. 'It's important, and we may uncover information pertinent to the death of Alan Miller.'

'I don't see any harm in it; as long as you share everything with me.'

'Can Flo tell us the results of the lab tests?'

George sighed.

'Okay, but don't tell anyone outside this room anything about the case. That includes your friends, Ghita and Roz. They're not exactly discreet.'

I couldn't disagree with him.

'Okay. It's a deal.'

George rubbed his chin.

'By the way, we found an empty Matlings' box in a rubbish bin down the street from the restaurant. I'm told it originally contained raw prawns. I'm not sure it's connected to Surfusion, but it seems logical. We are having it tested in the lab for fingerprints and residues.'

'Why would anyone dispose of the box so far from the kitchen?'

'We don't know yet, but Ed Murray has the contract to supply the restaurant with fish and crustaceans, so someone may have discarded the box outside the kitchen, to hide the origin of the prawns.'

'Matlings again,' said Harry. 'Something smells fishy.'

Chapter 18

The next day, I felt a little more cheerful about the prospects for a break in the Surfusion investigation. George had jumped the gun with his conclusions, but their discovery of a burner phone hidden in the toilet could only be a positive development. The fact that the fingerprint on the mobile phone chip did not belong to Miller made me sure he had been set up to take the fall by somebody else. The empty prawn box from Matlings had increased my suspicions about the couple. They had a grudge against Kieron and Rohan for not selecting them as the providers of the seafood for Surfusion. How far might they have gone to get their own back?

I opened the shop and sat at the counter doing the accounts. We were not exactly coining it in, but the Danish furniture had been a success and covered our costs for the month. Sales improved still further when Grace popped by to make me an offer for the curio cabinet I had bought at Shoreham. She ran her hand across the top and examined the price tag with her nose wrinkled in disgust.

'If I had arrived five minutes earlier, this would have been mine for half the price,' she said.

'You need a new alarm clock.'

'Max had other ideas.'

She blushed at her own confession. I laughed. She had become a lot more approachable since our brush with the world of witchcraft. I was about to ask her if she wanted a tea when my mobile phone pinged. A message from Ghita.

'Are you at the shop?'

'Yes, I'm here with Grace,' I texted back.

Ghita arrived almost instantaneously, pink cheeked with excitement, a sure sign of news. She gave me a fragrant hug and squeaked in my ear almost bursting my eardrum.

'We've been cleared.'

'Of what?' said Grace.

'The council's hygiene team has given the Surfusion a clean bill of health. We can reopen it once the police give us the go ahead.'

'I couldn't believe what happened to you,' said Grace. 'I'm so sorry. Imagine a famous food critic dying at your restaurant's opening night! What are the chances?'

'Oh, but he didn't. I mean it wasn't him. It was someone else,' I said.

'I don't understand.'

'What do you mean?' said Ghita. 'Are you saying it wasn't Leonard Black who died after all?'

'Let's have a cup of tea,' I said. 'There's been a lot of water under the bridge since it happened, and not all of it has been in teapots.'

We were soon sipping cups of hot jasmine tea upstairs. Grace looked around the café. I guessed she had hoped to get a slice of one of Ghita's delicious cakes. She liked the lemony ones best. She would wrap up an extra slice for her husband and take it back to Wong's Emporium with her. Ghita noticed her gaze.

'Oh, I must make a cake for the Vintage. I've been so preoccupied I couldn't face it, but I'm feeling better now.'

'I wish you would,' I said. 'My clients have been deserting me in droves and George is forced to eat chocolate croissants, poor man.'

'I second that,' said Grace. 'The Vintage is not the same without your cakes.'

Ghita glowed with pleasure.

'I'm still in the dark about the whole Leonard Black scenario,' said Ghita. 'Do you know anything you can tell me?'

I sighed. The police hadn't made any statements about the real identity of the man who died yet, but George had told us he would put out a statement soon.

'I will, but you have to promise me you'll keep it to yourself until the police statement comes out.'

'When will that be?'

'Today or tomorrow.'

'I can do that,' said Ghita.

'Who would I tell?' said Grace.

'True. Well, the man who died was not Leonard Black. In fact, no one is, but that's another story. The name of the man who died at Surfusion was Alan Miller. He worked for a company who hired out pranksters. Somebody paid him to go to there and pretend to be Leonard Black. We don't know what he planned to do, because something he ate gave him anaphylactic shock and he died before telling us.'

'Who would do such a thing?' said Ghita.

'We don't know, but it appears to be an act of sabotage intended to shut down the restaurant. The question is why? If we have the why, we will find the who.'

'Can I talk to Rohan and Kieron about this?' said Ghita. 'They may be able to help.'

'Not yet. Wait until George's team releases the statement. Isn't Kieron with his mother again?'

'Yes, she supposedly had a relapse. Rohan is also away. I think they needed time apart. The closure's been tough on their relationship.'

'I'm not surprised. All that work gone in an instant,' said Grace.

'There's another thing, also top secret,' I said. 'The police found an empty Matlings' box in a dustbin down the street from Surfusion.'

'But what has that got to do with anything?' said Ghita.

'The Matlings are the people who competed with Ed and Roz to supply seafood to Surfusion. They are highly competitive people who did not take their loss very well.'

'Are you saying the box contained something which killed Alan Miller?' said Grace.

'There's no proof of anything, but it seems like an odd coincidence. Who would dispose of the box containing raw prawns in the middle of the street? Unless they had already put them in a bowl or something?'

'Oh, I see what you mean,' said Grace.

'Did you see a Matlings box in the Surfusion kitchen?' I said.

'No, I don't think so, but I wasn't cooking the seafood. Maybe Kieron knows about it.'

'Can you let me know as soon as he's back in town? I really need to speak to him and Rohan about this. Someone is trying to sabotage the restaurant and we need to figure out who it is before somebody else gets hurt.'

'I promise.'

'What a strange thing to happen,' said Grace. 'The poor man who died may have been completely innocent.'

'He probably was,' I said. 'His girlfriend told me he was being paid triple to go off the books. He wasn't suicidal.'

'How depressing,' said Ghita. 'We definitely need more cakes to cheer ourselves up.'

'We could do with more exercise classes too,' said Grace. 'To raise our serotonin levels.'

'Well said. Come on, Ghita. Your public needs you. Helen and Joy have both been complaining since you stopped doing them. We all need a strenuous aerobics class followed by a session in the Shanty.'

'I'm not really in the mood,' said Ghita.

'That's because you have given no classes,' said Grace. 'It's a vicious circle.'

'I wish you would start them up again,' I said. 'My waistbands are all getting too tight.'

Ghita sighed, but her resistance lessened.

'I suppose I could rent the church hall again.'

'Fair's fair. I told you secret information. The least you can do is reciprocate with a class. You'll get paid too, which is more than I do for all my sleuthing.'

'You love investigating. You don't need to get paid.'

'And you used to love running Fat Fighters, so what's changed?' said Grace.

Ghita shrugged.

'Nothing. I'll organise a class and let everyone know on the WhatsApp group.'

'And let me know when the boys are back in town too,' I said.

'I promise. The minute they arrive.'

Chapter 19

The next morning, I walked to Second Home along the promenade, enjoying the gentle warmth generated by the sun. Fluffy white clouds bombed across the sky, but the breeze at ground level hardly lifted the flags from their poles. Herbert had been absent from the shelter the last few times I looked for him. I suspected he had found a Mrs Herbert to keep him occupied with domestic chores like building a nest and shrieking duets from the rooftops. No doubt I would see him again when pickings became scarce after the disappearance of migratory birds like the lesser-spotted day-tripper. I had not generated any leads for my investigation in my sleep and I had awoken grumpy with dissatisfaction. I breathed in a lungful of seaweed redolent air and let it out slowly, blowing my problems into the open sea.

I opened the shop and peered around, noting the even coating of dust which had settled on all the tabletops and shelves. At this time of year, the café upstairs spent all day flooded in sunlight, but the ground floor only occasionally emerged from shadow. I peered across the road at the Surfusion and thought about poor Alan Miller. Then I realised I had not spoken to his fiancée, Susanne Jones, since we had been to visit her. I scrolled through my contacts and found her mobile number.

'Hello, Susanne? It's Tanya Bowe. We came to see you in your flat after poor Alan died.'

'Oh, hi Tanya. Of course I remember.'

'I wondered how you were. Have the police been keeping you up to date with the investigation?'

'Not really. I expect they're too busy, and I'm not family.'

Her voice caught in her throat and my heart went out to her.

'I can tell you what happened if you would like.'

'Would you? It's the not knowing that's difficult.'

'Well, it's been confirmed that he died of anaphylactic shock. We're not sure what he ate yet, but, unfortunately, the fact he had asthma may have caused it to be fatal.'

'I don't understand. What about his EpiPen?'

'I don't know why it didn't work. My ex-husband George did CPR on him, but he couldn't save him. I'm so terribly sorry.'

'Oh, it's not your fault. It's just weird. He was so careful about what he ate.'

'I spoke to the people who run the restaurant. They assured me there were no peanuts anywhere near the kitchen. They are struggling to deal with the closure and Alan's death. It's been hard on them.'

'I can imagine. Alan would never have wanted to cause harm to anyone. He would have been devastated by the result of his prank. I hope they can recover.'

'The local council had closed the restaurant. They needed to run a full safety check before it was possible to reopen. My friend Ghita told me they have given it the all clear now.'

'That's good news at least. And all because of a prank. I can't believe it.'

'I'm so sorry to be the bearer of bad news. Please call me if you need anything.'

'I will. Thank you for thinking of me. Life will never be the same again, but Harry made me believe I can carry on. Tell him thank you.'

Afterwards, I looked up the florist nearest to her flat and ordered an enormous bunch of sunflowers for her from Harry and me. I hoped they would bring some well-needed sunshine into her life. I couldn't imagine losing Harry, especially in such a bizarre fashion. All those clichés about making the most of every day are true.

The doorbell clanged as Mouse and Leanne arrived looking sheepish. I almost rolled my eyes at their embarrassment. It's only sex, for heaven's sake. It's not like they murdered someone. Mouse set about dusting the downstairs furniture, and I sent Leanne out to buy supplies of milk and chocolate croissants. Ghita had promised to bake us a cake, but I wouldn't hold my breath. I understood her struggle to return to normality, but my clients at the Vintage had begun to grumble. I hoped a chocolate croissant would sweeten the blow of yet another day without one of Ghita's special bakes. I couldn't wait for Kieron and Rohan to get back to Seacastle for questioning. I needed to get to the bottom of this case before we lost both Surfusion and our supply of cakes for good.

The shop door opened, and Roz entered, giving me a big hug. She held on longer than usual when I remained rigid with stress, forcing me to yield to her generous spirit.

'What's up with you then?' she said. 'Still fretting about Surfusion? Haven't you made any progress with the investigation?'

I sighed.

'Sort of, but every time I make progress in one direction, another possibility raises its head. A young man is dead, but seemingly by accident. Why would someone want to sabotage the opening night of a new restaurant? If I could figure out the reason for that, I might be able to find the culprit.'

'You'll get there in the end. You always do. Is there anything I can research for you? I—'

In that moment, Leanne came back in with the supplies for the Vintage. She glanced at Roz without recognition and went upstairs. Roz turned to me, her mouth open in shock.

'What is she doing here?'

'Leanne? She works, worked, at the Surfusion. She's helping Mouse in the Vintage until they re-open it.'

She shook her head.

'You don't know, do you?'

'What don't I know?'

Roz lowered her voice to a whisper.

'Leanne's father is Keith Matling, the fisherman. She's probably spying on you.'

I couldn't believe my ears.

'Don't be ridiculous. Why would she do that?'

'You're so naïve sometimes. Who let her work at the Surfusion? You've been conned. She's the prime suspect for sabotage there, if you ask me.'

'Leanne? She wouldn't say boo to a goose.'

Despite my panic, the logic of what she had said penetrated my brain. I felt doubt seeping in. Why would Keith Matling's daughter be working at the Surfusion anyway? Could it have something to do with Alan Miller's odd appearance? I couldn't imagine anyone killing someone over a lost order. And then I remembered the Matlings' prawn box George's team had found in the rubbish bin. Would they find Leanne's fingerprints all over it? I didn't want to jump to conclusions and upset Leanne unnecessarily. She had been struggling since the night of the death and only perked up when Mouse was around. I needed to find out if Ed had anything to do with the box first. After all, he supplied the restaurant. Perhaps he had improvised because of a shortage? It seemed unlikely, but then everything seemed unlikely about this investigation.

'Let's go upstairs and find out,' said Roz.

I grabbed her arm, preventing her from stomping up the stairs.

'Can you not say anything to Leanne just yet?' I said. 'I'd rather she doesn't know we rumbled her. I must check something with Ed first.'

Roz raised an eyebrow.

'Seriously? Not everyone is happy to tolerate a cuckoo in the nest.'

'We don't know she is one. She doesn't use Keith's surname. Maybe she's oblivious to the feud.'

'I'll take your word for it. Ed's at sea, but he'll be back shortly. Shall I tell him to drop in this afternoon?'

'That would be great if he can manage it. Otherwise, tomorrow will be fine.'

I tried to behave normally with Leanne for the rest of the day, but I'm not a talented actress. Mouse picked up my obvious discomfort and imagined it to result from them coming in with bedheads. I caught him glaring at me, but I did not want to share the real reason for my disquiet until I knew the truth behind Leanne's deception. They tidied up after the last customer in the Vintage and left early without asking me if they could go. I felt terrible, but I didn't want to warn Mouse before I found out the truth. He could over-react sometimes and I didn't want to be on the receiving end of his wrath.

Ed breezed in at closing time. He hugged Roz and greeted me without approaching. I couldn't imagine what Roz had said to make him this cagey. Usually, I got a hug too.

'So what's the big mystery?' he said. 'Roz tells me you want to question me about the Surfusion murder.'

'I wouldn't put it that way,' I said. 'The police found something odd near the restaurant and I wanted to ask you about it.'

'Fire away.'

'It's a little awkward.'

'More awkward than a dead body on opening night?'

I laughed.

'No. I suppose not. How well do you get on with Keith Matling?'

'We used to bump along okay, for rivals, but recently... Well, you know I won the contract for Surfusion? That's made it more difficult.'

'Would you ask him for help if you hadn't got the stock Kieron requested?'

'Is this about the scallops?'

'What scallops?'

'Kieron had a hissy fit, because I couldn't provide scallops for opening night. He had to change the menu at the last minute. I've never seen such a scene over such a small thing.'

'What did you provide instead?'

'King prawns. Big fresh ones for a ceviche, as requested.'

'And where did you get them?'

'From my nets.'

'Nowhere else?'

'Are you suggesting I stole them?'

'Of course not. I need to know.'

'You should tell us why,' said Roz.

George will kill me.

'The police found a discarded Matlings' prawn box in a rubbish bin near Surfusion.'

'You're asking me if I gave Kieron some of Matling's prawns without telling him? The answer's no. Of course not. I would have had to explain why half the

118

prawns were not fresh. Matling freezes most of his shellfish.' Ed scratched his head. 'What's this all about, anyway? I heard the man's death was an accident.'

'It may have been, but the sabotage wasn't. Someone is trying to destroy the reputation of Surfusion before they ever get going.'

'And you suspect me? That's rich. I'd be thrilled if they were successful. After all, they're buying their fish from me.'

'I don't suspect you, Ed. I'm trying to find out if a stray box of prawns can lead us to the perpetrators of this prank gone wrong, or if it's merely a red herring.'

Ed laughed.

'Now that's one thing I don't sell. Maybe you should find out if the box is related to the crime or not first?'

'Maybe I should.'

Chapter 20

Ed's visit did not remove the shadow of suspicion from Leanne's shoulders, but for some reason, I still felt unwilling to confront her about her presence at Surfusion. I went home to the Grotty Hovel and brooded in my room, pretending to read a book. I wrote lists of scenarios for the evening of the opening, some of which included Leanne as a chief protagonist of the disaster and others which did not. I always ended up at the same sticking point – the death of Alan Miller. Until I knew how he had died, I could not progress. I fell asleep despite the wind rattling my windows, dreaming of human-sized crustaceans invading Seacastle and clacking their claws in some sort of weird morse code. It reminded me of an old episode of Doctor Who, or was it Star Trek?

The next day, I fed Hades to shut him up and sulked in the kitchen after burning the toast and letting my tea go cold. Mouse had not appeared. I didn't know if he had come home or not, but I suspected the latter. Even two fresh slices of toast slathered in butter and honey couldn't lift me far out of my slump. I took out my notebook and reread my latest musings on the investigation, getting butter stains on the pages. Why had Alan Miller sent back the main course half-eaten? I made a new entry to remind me to ask Ghita about it.

As I procrastinated, my mobile phone pinged at me, and I checked the screen. A message from Flo informed me she expected the results from most of the laboratory tests that afternoon. I felt a frisson of excitement. Surely they would bring us closer to the truth of what happened that evening? Placing my cup in the sink, I headed for the front door. It's not like I had any choice about opening Second Home, as I needed the money. Raindrops streamed down the windowpanes as a large black cloud dropped its contents on the town. I felt as if the damp had penetrated my bones, taking away my energy and fogging my brain. I forced myself to put on a raincoat and dig out an umbrella, with the promise of a nice frothy latte as soon as I got to work. I trotted down the pavement and jumped into the Mini before I could get wet.

Sometimes, heavy rain can be your friend. I managed to park in the side street nearest to my shop because of the total population of Seacastle staying at home to have a second cup of tea rather than venture out into the deluge. I glanced at the Surfusion restaurant across the street and spotted someone gazing in through the windows. There wasn't much to see in there. The police had piled all the tables on top of each other during their searches and the taxidermy fish stared goggle-eyed out from the walls into the gloom. The man turned around and saw me watching him. He lifted a tentative hand to wave at me and I returned the gesture. He came across the road in a few strides, leaping the huge puddle which had gathered on the road. As he approached me, I wondered if I should recognise him. He had the confident air of a handsome man who was used to getting his own way. He was impeccably dressed. Was he a tv star?

'Hello,' he said. 'I heard they killed someone. I hope they closed the restaurant for good?'

'I'm not sure they have. The police are still working on the case.'

His brow furrowed.

'Didn't the food kill him?'

'Nobody knows yet,' I said. 'And you are?'

'Oh, I should have said. I'm Leonard Black.'

I may have gasped. I recovered and shook his hand, trying to behave normally.

'The restaurant critic?'

He smiled. I realised his smug look came from his assumption I was star-struck, not that I knew about his link to the death at Surfusion. He tilted his head to one side.

'You've heard of me then?'

'Um, yes, but—'

'Reports of my death have been greatly exaggerated,' he said. 'I wondered if your café might be open yet. I'm in need of a cappuccino.'

'Sure. I'm not open yet, so it'll take me a few minutes to get everything switched on. You can look at our stock while you're waiting if you get bored.'

'I don't buy secondhand furniture,' he said, and followed me inside.

I showed him up the stairs and offered him a window seat before retreating into the kitchenette on the ground floor. My mood had not improved after his dismissal of my shop, but if I kept him there, I could at least get reinforcements. I sent George a frantic text message, alerting him to the presence of Black, and then went back upstairs with the milk. Black seemed to be fixated on scrolling through his phone, his expressions varying from gloating to amused to eye-rolling. I ground some coffee beans and made the coffee before adding the milk. There were so many questions I wanted to ask him; I didn't know where to start.

In the end, I blurted out 'Have you spoken to the police?'.

He raised an eyebrow.

'And why would I want to do that?' he said. 'Do I look like a criminal?'

'The man who died at the opening of the Surfusion restaurant impersonated you in order to get an invitation. I expect they would like to find out where you were at the time.'

'He did what? The news omitted that. The articles only reported the death of a man at a restaurant opening. I had no idea. I've been on holiday with my wife for two weeks. We were in danger of divorcing because of my obsession with my blog. She gave me an ultimatum; either the phone went off, or I did. I left it at home.'

'What about the review on your blog?'

He frowned.

'You seem to know rather a lot about the incident for a shopkeeper. Are you the town gossip?'

'My partner and I were there on the night. My son works as a waiter at Surfusion. My ex-husband is investigating the death of the impersonator. And I'm a private investigator.'

'A snoop? Why are you interested?'

'I'm trying to find out why someone is attempting to shut down Surfusion. It belongs to my friends.'

'Your friends? Those two losers?'

He snorted and finished his coffee. I was reminded of my mother's comment about handsome men containing ugly contents.

'And why are you so interested?' I asked. 'If you didn't know about the imitator already?'

'Somebody hacked my blog while I was away and left a vitriolic review for Surfusion. I wanted to see the restaurant with my own eyes. Professional curiosity, you understand. I found myself in the area and I wanted to examine the scene of the culinary crime. It's a pity they had to close down. This end of town is a dump. It could have done with a decent place to eat.'

It's true that the west end of Seacastle lacks grace and has too many charity shops and barbers, but I bristled at his dismissal of my street.

'They haven't closed down. The council's health and safety team has done a thorough review of the place to find out what happened. There's no evidence to suggest the man died because of the food. He may have had a heart attack.'

'Wasn't he too young for one of those?'

'I guess the autopsy will tell us that. Is it possible to find out who left the review?'

'I don't know. I've talked to the web developer. He took down the review for me as soon as I realised the link with the death at Surfusion. He has also increased security on the site. I would never have made such a scene, or published such an unprofessional piece of journalism. I have my standards.'

The doorbell clanged downstairs, and I heard George puffing up the stairs with PC Joe Brennan. Leonard Black stood up when they appeared.

'I'll be going now,' he said. 'How much was the coffee?'

'I'm Detective Inspector George Carter, and this is Acting Detective Constable Joe Brennan. I'd like to speak to you about an incident at the Surfusion restaurant which resulted in the death of a young man.'

'Am I under arrest?'

'No. We'd like you to help us with our inquiries. Your name was used to gain access to the opening night there. We'd like to clear up the reasons behind it.'

'Well, if I'm not under arrest, I'm not interested in helping. My entire existence depends on my anonymity. I have no intention of having my real identity revealed just to help you with your inquiries. You'll have to excuse me.'

He pushed past George and Joe and descended the stairs two at a time. George stared after him, open-mouthed. Joe swore and then apologised to me. I smirked as a revelation hit me.

'He didn't pay for his coffee,' I said.

'Honestly, Tan, why is that relevant?' said George.

'I'd like to report a theft. That man ran away without paying.'

'Oh, I see,' said Joe, grinning too.

'Are you two completely mad?' said George. 'He is a person of extreme interest in this investigation, and he's just disappeared again. It's a disaster.'

'Shall I tell him?' said Joe. 'Or would you like to?'

'Oh, I think I shall.'

I thought George would explode.

'Tell me what?' he said, crimson with frustration.

'The man who stole my coffee left his fingerprints on my mug.'

'We can't use his fingerprints. He hasn't been charged with anything. Be serious, Tan, if you can.'

'But—'

'We've got better things to do.'

His reaction though disappointing, was not unexpected. George had never been keen on ideas that didn't come from him.

'How about a coffee?' I said.

Chapter 21

George never turned down a coffee, but he looked pointedly at Joe Brennan who shrugged and grinned at me.

'I'd better get back to the station,' he said.

'Won't you have a coffee yourself?' I asked.

'No thanks. I've got a load of paperwork to complete. The DI will take your statement.'

He gave me a nod and made his way out of the shop, stopping to pick up and examine a pretty, bright blue, cloisonne box I had on the counter. I wondered who he had in mind when he did this. Joe remained an enigma despite being on the edges of our circle since he first joined the force. Perhaps his mother or a girlfriend? Sally Wright at the station reception would know. Roz would soon find out from her if I asked.

George took out his notebook. He made some notes while I prepared him a coffee. I moved the cup from the table by nudging it onto a tray without George noticing my unwillingness to touch it. I left it on the side for later. George looked into the display cabinet we used for cakes and biscuits.

'What? No cake?' he said. 'That's a tragedy if I ever saw one.'

'Ghita is not in the mood.'

'I can't say I'm surprised. This whole scenario must be messing with her head.'

His phone emitted a buzz, and he picked it up to glance at the screen. The message made him pump his fist.

'Yes! The results are in,' he said. 'Flo's on her way to the station. Shall I tell her to drop in for a coffee? I'll have a preliminary chat with her and you can eavesdrop.'

'Really? That would be fantastic.'

'Fair's fair. I wouldn't have met the real Leonard Black if it wasn't for you. We'll track him down. Can you please buy us something sweet to go with our coffees? I've got cake withdrawal symptoms.'

While George diverted Flo via the Vintage, I walked to the bakery and bought a selection of croissants. The smell of buttery, flaky pastry made me feel delirious with sugar cravings. I chose chocolate and almond filled ones, and a couple of plain ones for people without a sweet tooth. I cradled the warm paper bag on my way back to the shop, inhaling the divine smells which escaped from it. When I could bear it no longer, I reached in and broke off the corner of an almond croissant and bit into it. I stopped to enjoy the sensation of the almond paste on my tongue.

'Are those for me?' said a voice I knew well.

Flo.

'Maybe. If you tell me everything you know,' I said.

'Hm. I'm not sure if George will like that. Let's negotiate.'

Flo and I walked back to the shop, sharing the almond croissant. George looked up as we came into the Vintage.

'Hey, you started without me,' he said.

'No, we didn't,' said Flo.

'What about those crumbs all over your jumpers?'

'Oh, the croissant. You can tell he's a detective,' I said.

'Hand them over,' said George, grabbing the bag and shoving his nose into it. 'Wow, those smell good!'

I made Flo and myself a latte and then waited with bated breath as she munched a couple of pastries with George. He glanced at me perched on the edge of my seat and laughed.

'Put the poor woman out of her misery,' he said. 'What does the lab say about our victim's stomach contents?'

'It's the most extraordinary result,' said Flo. 'I don't come close to understanding what's going on here. First, the victim had peanut powder in his stomach.'

'Which explains the anaphylactic reaction,' said George. 'But why didn't the EpiPen work?'

'The contents were denatured,' said Flo. 'I've no idea why.'

'Denatured? That's bizarre,' I said. 'Maybe it got left on a radiator or something.'

'Not as bizarre as the second ingredient. The victim's stomach contents were swimming in laxative.'

'Laxative? How on earth?' said George. 'Is laxative dangerous?'

'Not to my knowledge,' said Flo. 'But he ingested it at the restaurant.'

'Can we link the agents to any of the dishes?' said George.

'I was getting to that,' said Flo, chewing the end of her pen. 'They traced the source of the peanut powder to the ceviche.'

'The ceviche? But I had ceviche. It was delicious.'

'Ah, but you're not allergic to peanuts,' said Flo. 'Our victim was. It was pure good fortune that none of the other diners who ordered ceviche had peanut allergies too.'

'Somebody laced the ceviche with peanut powder? Why would they do that? It seems so random,' said George.

'Totally. Whoever did this counted on causing a ruckus. I doubt very much they intended to kill anyone,' said Flo.

'The contamination must have been an intentional part of the sabotage on opening night,' I said. 'But what if the saboteur knew about Miller's allergy? He can't have expected him to die, but he took an enormous risk.'

'They obviously didn't count on our victim having asthma as well. The combination killed him.'

Flo sighed.

'But the big mystery is the laxative. We only found traces in one bowl with traces of moules. The one served to the victim. Laxative would not have harmed him in the slightest, although he would have had terrible diarrhoea.'

Somewhere in my head a light went on. A very dim light. I said nothing, but I had an inkling of the source of the laxative. Since it was almost certainly unrelated to the sabotage or the death of the victim, I kept my thoughts to myself.

'Could the peanut powder have been hidden inside the prawns?' said George.

'Relatively easily,' said Flo.

I saw his expression harden.

'That box,' he said. 'I told you it was the key. Somebody used the Matlings' box to bring the prawns into the restaurant and then discarded the box outside so nobody would know.'

Flo stared at the screen and scrolled through her report.

'I don't have the results back from the box yet,' she said.

'We need to check it for peanut residue and fingerprints, asap,' said George. 'This is looking like manslaughter at the very least.'

'Finally,' said Flo. 'Now we're getting somewhere. That poor young man will get justice if I've anything to do with it.'

'What about the laxative?' said George.

I bit my lip. Come clean.

'I have a theory about the laxative,' I said. 'I think it's completely unrelated to the sabotage. Whoever introduced it into the bowl of moules was not targeting the victim. Can I do some checking? I promise to let you know the results.'

'It sounds more like another prank,' said Flo. 'But that makes me think of the victim's job. Are you sure it's not related?'

'As sure as I can be,' I said.

'Okay. I'll buy it. Let me know what you find out,' said George. 'I'll get the team to find out where the box came from.'

I had a horrible feeling that Leanne's fingerprints would be found on the box, and I wanted to question her before the police got hold of her. Since she was technically still a child at seventeen, they couldn't interview her without her parents present, and I could imagine how that would go. She might talk to me if Mouse was present, and I couldn't believe she would have adulterated the prawns of her own volition. We were missing pieces of the jigsaw, and I thought I knew where to look.

When George had left, I used a pencil to lift the cup and place it in a Ziplock bag. I hid it under the counter in case it came in useful later. Leonard Black, or whatever his name was, could easily be involved somehow. I didn't like his attitude at all. But maybe that's why he seemed suspicious. People who got up my nose always moved up my list of suspects. The truth was the Matlings had means and motive, and with Leanne working at Surfusion, they also had the opportunity. It was time to find out why she had lied to us.

Chapter 22

To my intense frustration, Leanne disappeared off the radar for a few days and wouldn't answer Mouse's text messages. Without her cooperation, the investigation stalled. The police finally gave the go-ahead for the re-opening of the Surfusion, but neither Kieron nor Rohan rushed back. I guessed they were at a loss about how to restart after such a disaster, or deciding if they even wanted to try. Ghita arrived at Second Home with a white chocolate and raspberry cake for our cabinet, but the promised exercise class did not materialise. I busied myself replacing sold furniture from the Vintage with pieces from the ground floor. The Vintage looked great, but I needed to replenish our stock. Luckily, Harry came up trumps with a clearance and I leapt at the chance to escape for a day.

Mouse sulked when I left him in charge, but he cheered up when Roz arrived bursting with gossip from around the town. She had the most uncanny ability to pick up the most obscure facts and string them together to make scandal. She would have won a gold medal at the scurrilous Olympiad. Harry honked his horn outside on the High Street and I grabbed my handbag. Mouse stood at the door to see me off and I kissed his forehead and stroked his black curls.

'Have fun with Roz,' I said. 'Don't forget to gather all the juiciest bits of gossip for me and Harry to hear tonight.'

'I will. Don't spend all my computer money.'

I bounced across the pavement and into a wall of sound in the new van. Harry had installed the old tape deck on the dashboard and he had put on a Pearl Jam tape.

'Welcome to paradise,' he said, giving me a soft kiss. 'I am your DJ for the day. What would madam like to hear?'

'This is pretty good. Why don't we leave it on? Where are we going today?'

'Outside Arundel. We're clearing out a church.'

'A church or a vicarage?'

'Both, I think. The vicar has died and they're combining the parishes. The bishop is selling the vicarage to raise funds to repair the church in the next village. I think the church will also become a house or a pub or something like that.'

It didn't take us long to arrive at Arundel. The castle caught my eye with its ancient keep looming from the motte in the centre surrounded by the curtain wall of the castle. The tall Barbican was built just after the battle of Hastings, and I wished we had time to take in the fabulous views from the top. Instead, we sped out of town, hugging the hedgerows and heading for a nearby village containing the church and vicarage, which we had been contracted to clear. The hedgerows were bulging with new leaves and buds which camouflaged the myriad nests hiding within. We pulled up beside the vicarage, leaving enough room for cars to pass, and jumped out.

'Wow, that's a pretty house. It's a pity we can't afford something like that,' said Harry.

'I expect it will be bought by some Londoner as a holiday home,' said a voice.

I turned to see a rotund man with a tonsure standing beside the van. He had materialised out of thin air, which I found a little unnerving. Harry approached him and shook his hand.

'You're doing the clearance?' he said. 'I never thought I'd see the day when they sold our vicarage and the church. It's a sad indictment of the modern era. Nobody goes to church anymore. They all worship Mammon instead.'

'I'm Harry Fletcher and this is my partner, Tanya Bowe. And you are?'

'Fineas Goulding, verger, late of this parish.'

He bit his lip. I couldn't think of anything to say. Clearances were sad occasions for lots of reasons, and many of them signified the end of an era, but it seemed incorrect to point this out to a man who thought Christianity was the era that was ending.

'Should we take everything?' said Harry.

'You might as well. They've done that to us already. The Church is open too. I'll shut up later.'

He shuffled away, his bald head shining in the sun. I felt a wave of sympathy for him.

'Come on, Miz Bowe. We've got work to do,' said Harry.

We walked up the cobbled path to the front door and pushed it open. The downstairs rooms contained a host of well-worn chairs and sofas covered in a riot of pink chintz sitting on ancient Persian rugs faded from years of exposure to sunlight. The seats had the potential to be re-upholstered and reinforced in Tommy's workshop in London, but were too far gone for my shop. I spotted a pair of framed embroideries hanging on either side of the tiled fireplace featuring large bunches of rhododendrons and peonies in art deco vases. I fell in love in an instant as I could picture them in the Grotty Hovel on either side of my fireplace. I took them down along with the slightly foxed mirror hanging between them.

Harry wandered upstairs and I could hear the floorboards protesting as he paced through the bedrooms, examining their contents. He didn't call me up, so I knew there probably wouldn't be anything to interest me upstairs. I moved through the small sitting room to a piece of furniture which had been covered with an old sheet. My pulse quickened as I took in the rounded shape at the top. I pulled the sheet away and revealed an Arts and Crafts oak roll-top desk. Its dark varnish had lightened over the years and now it shone honey-coloured at me. I opened and shut some drawers, which had all been emptied except for one. It contained a hymn book, fat with dried flowers inserted in between its pages. I took it out and removed the elastic band, holding it shut. I flicked through it. Primroses and bluebells and daisies from summers past lay flattened and dry, but still bright, inside it. Who had put all this care into preserving these flowers and then abandoned them in this drawer? Perhaps the vicar's wife? I put the elastic band back on the book and put it into my handbag.

I went upstairs and helped Harry to bring down a couple of bedframes and two small chests of drawers. There were also two papier-mâché wastepaper bins made from scraps of magazines and painted with clear varnish. I often wished I had the patience to do crafting, but I always seemed to have something else to do. I had tried decoupage in the past, but my impatience meant I always had bubbles in my resin or wrinkles in my napkins. Perhaps when I got older, I would develop patience? It seemed unlikely. People are supposed to mellow when they get older, but most people I know became markedly more grumpy and less tolerant of fools.

I showed Harry the desk, and he beamed at me.

'That's a corker,' he said. 'I can see it in the Grotty Hovel.'

'But it's worth quite a bit,' I said. 'I can't justify keeping it.'

'Why don't you just hold on to it for a while? You can always put it in the shop when you get bored with it.'

'In two hundred years' time?'

'Whenever.'

'But I want to keep the embroidered pictures too, And the papier- mâché wastepaper bins. I was supposed to restock the shop.'

'What about the small chests of drawers? And there's a set of kitchen chairs in the larder. Nice sturdy ones with wicker seats.'

'You don't mind?'

'Why would I mind? Seeing you happy is the only thing I care about. Tommy will buy all the upholstered stuff. That will pay for petrol.'

'But what about your bills?'

'I've only been home once this month to cannibalise the tape deck from the old van.'

He rubbed his chin.

'I was thinking. Well, it seems pointless to run two households. Why don't I let my house out and move in to the Grotty Hovel full time?'

My heart skipped a beat. I tried to be nonchalant.

'If that's what you want,' I said. 'After all, Mouse will go to university soon, so I'll need someone to wash up the dishes.'

'Is that all you've got to say?'

'Um, well, you could hoover as well if you want.'

He roared with laughter.

'You are the least romantic person I have ever met in my entire life.'

'I try.'

'Come here, you silly woman.'

He enveloped me in his muscly arms and stared into my eyes. I could see constellations and fireworks and eternity in his. He lowered his lips onto mine and I shut my eyes. I don't know how long we stood there, but it felt like infinity.

'Let's go home then,' he said.

Mouse rolled his eyes when we turned up with the new furniture for the Grotty Hovel. Harry tripped over Hades as he helped Mouse bring in the roll-top desk, causing him to yowl and dash outside. He refused to come back in, even when I tried to bribe him with pieces of cold lamb. I put them in his bowl, knowing he would not resist for long. The two framed embroideries looked spectacular over the fireplace as I knew they would, and the desk fitted in the space previously occupied by the drop-leaf pine table which we transferred to the van for selling. Mouse put his hands on his hips.

'No wonder you make no money,' he said. 'Anything nice gets hoarded at the Grotty Hovel.'

'I have a confession to make,' I said.

'Something else you want to keep here?' said Mouse.

'Um, you could say that.'

'Do we have enough room? What is it?'

'Me,' said Harry, his voice high. 'Is that okay with you?'

Mouse let out a yelp and grabbed Harry in a bear hug, his eyes glistening.

'Really?' he said, over Harry's shoulder. 'Harry's moving in?'

'If you don't mind,' I said.

Mouse did not answer. He hugged Harry closer. I had a massive lump in my throat. Some things just feel right.

Chapter 23

My sister Helen could not contain her excitement when she found out Harry had moved into the Grotty Hovel full time. She loved happy endings. She wouldn't watch a film, or read a book, unless she had the guarantee of a happily ever-after. I suspected she longed for George to get on one knee and produce a box from his jacket pocket containing a one-carat diamond. I had not told her the unvarnished truth about him. George had the romantic attributes of a breeze block and had a well-deserved reputation for being a miser. In our former lives, he had persuaded me to marry him by explaining how much money we would save if we tied the knot. I must admit that I could not claim to be much better in the romance stakes.

Harry made all the running in our relationship. His army background had made him excellent at hiding his feelings, but he had a soft heart under the rufty-tufty exterior. I hoped we could compromise on our share of the limited space at the Grotty Hovel. I had a feeling I would have to tolerate Harry's taxidermy pike in pride of place on the dresser. He rang the estate agent to put the house on the rental market and the broker advised him to leave it partially furnished. He took advantage of his decision to offload some of his unwanted bits by adding them to the load for Tommy. He took off to London with a van of furniture later that week, leaving me at work. I moved the furniture aside on the ground floor and waxed the boards first thing before I opened up the shop. The floor polisher bumped over the uneven floor and buffed the wax to a shine, sending vibrations up my arms. When I had finished, I wound the flex back onto the holders and placed it into the kitchen cupboard under the stairs.

As I came back to the counter, I noticed Leanne loitering on the pavement and called her into the shop. Mouse had gone to the phone shop to upgrade the memory for his phone. I had pretended I knew what that meant. He had laughed at me and gone whistling down the High Street. I had a pang of misery as I imagined him gone to study for the term. Leanne came into the shop with a smile, but she seemed nervous. She kept glancing at the door and fidgeting. Maybe she had not told her parents about helping me in the shop. I felt pretty sure they wouldn't approve. Might she be worried about somebody spotting her?

'Hi there. Mouse will be back soon I expect. Do you fancy giving me a hand?'

She relaxed a little, oblivious to the ambush I had planned. I did not pin her down immediately. I asked her to help me polish the tabletops in the Vintage and reattach some price tags. The shop smelled of polish and coffee, guaranteed to enthuse the punters. And Ghita's fresh cake would tempt them to stay awhile. We finished our task and made a pot of tea. She did not appear keen to sit with me at the table. I wondered if she expected me to interrogate her about Surfusion. Had she realised I had discovered her secret? I sat back in my chair, sipping my tea. The silence seemed to unnerve her. She dropped her spoon on the floor and it reminded me of her reaction to the presence of her mother in my shop. I saw a way in.

'You're quite young to have moved out of the family home,' I said. 'Do you live by yourself? Or do you have flatmates?'

'I live with my sister.'

'That's nice. Don't you get on with your parents?'

She frowned.

'Not really. They are always telling me what to do.'

'What does your father do for a living?'

'He's a fishmonger. He has a shop at Shoreham.'

'Matlings? That's a fantastic place. It's like the Noah's Ark of fish.'

She shrugged.

'I guess.'

'How come you were working at Surfusion?'

Her eyes narrowed, and she looked like her mother.

'What do you mean? There's not exactly a ton of work around here you know.'

'It seems like a strange place to choose, after Kieron picked the Murrays to supply the fish. I heard your father had words with him.'

'I'm sure he did. Dad thinks everybody in West Sussex should buy their seafood from him. But that's nothing to do with me.'

'I've been trying to figure out what happened to that poor young man. Can you tell me what happened on the day of the opening?'

'I didn't see any of it. I was in the kitchen washing the plates the whole evening.'

'I meant earlier on.'

She fiddled with her spoon, threatened to drop it again.

'What's that got to do with his death?'

'The police found an empty prawn box from your father's shop in a bin down the street. I don't suppose you know anything about that.'

Her eyes opened wide, and she stood up. I blocked the stairs.

'I don't want to call the police, but they took your fingerprints to eliminate you from enquiries. Are they going to find them on the box too?'

She sat down again. I waited.

'It's not what it looks like.'

'I'm sure you have a reasonable explanation, but you need to tell me if we're going to work out what happened that night.'

'I was working in the kitchen stacking up the plates and there was a knock on the back door. The others were having a staff meeting in the restaurant, discussing the menu and taking orders and so on, so I went to open it.'

'Who was it?'

'I didn't recognise him. I think he's a taxi driver. He gave me the box of prawns and told me Kieron had ordered them for the ceviche.'

'What did you do?'

'I thanked him and went to store them in the fridge. I couldn't find any room for the box, so I added them to the Tupperware container with the other prawns. I forgot to mention it to anyone. I didn't think it was that important. But then...'

She trailed off and sobbed. I moved to her side and put an arm around her shoulders.

'You're doing brilliantly. Tell me what happened next.'

'We were so busy all afternoon. I completely forgot about the prawns. Then people started arriving, and we were all at full stretch for the whole evening. I remember Kieron losing it when Ghita took the moules out to Leonard Black, and then the horrible review came up on the blog and all hell broke out. We heard screaming from the restaurant and Mouse told us Leonard Black had collapsed. Kieron was shouting about something in the food being responsible. He got completely hysterical and cried. I remembered about the prawns and started panicking in case they caused the collapse. I was worried that my father had sent the box as revenge for not being chosen to supply the restaurant. I couldn't believe he would do anything harmful, but I had to protect him. He's my father after all. When no-one was looking, I fished the Matling box out of the rubbish bin and hid it in my bag. I kept it until we could go home when I dropped it into a litter bin on the High Street. I thought nobody would notice.' She wiped her eyes and lifted her head. 'Were they poisoned? The prawns? I'll never forgive myself if I killed somebody.'

'No, they weren't. It's possible some of them contained peanut powder, but we don't know yet. The box is at the laboratory for testing right now. They will also find your fingerprints on it, so you may have to tell the police about this eventually, but you don't have to worry, because your parents can sit in the interview with you.'

'But what if they're the ones who sent the box to Surfusion?' she said, sniffing.

I hadn't thought of that. They definitely had a motive to disrupt opening night. Nobody could have foreseen the death of Alan Miller/Leonard Black. I would have to tell George about this.

'I don't know. I'm sure whoever did this didn't intend to kill anyone, just cause a scene. It's not your fault. You had no way of knowing about the contamination. The police will understand.'

But would they? Leanne's parents had a reputation for being over competitive and unscrupulous when it came to business. Had they overstepped the mark this time? Was Leanne even telling me the truth about her involvement? At least Ed Murray was out of the frame for the time being. George would have to deal with the Matlings. I was out of my league.

Chapter 24

Leanne left soon after talking to me. She told me to tell Mouse to come and see her at the flat later on. She had been grey-faced with worry when she left. I rang George and told him about my conversation. He did not interrupt me except to prompt me for extra details. I could almost hear the cogs whirring in his head. The one impressive aspect of George's detective work is his insistence on evidence before he will act. He had been waiting for a reason to see the Matlings, and now he had one.

I asked him to talk to them before he interviewed Leanne. She did not appear to have a motive to sabotage the Surfusion, but people lie all the time. What if her parents had asked or persuaded her to mix the rogue prawns in with the fresh ones from Ed? What if there was no taxi driver but her own father handing her the box? Presumably, her father's fingerprints would also be on the box if this was so. George promised to ensure that all prints on the box were checked and double checked before he made his mind up. The taxi driver's prints would also need to be checked before he was eliminated. With so many people pretending to be somebody they weren't, I felt like my brains had been mixed with a whisk.

When Mouse arrived, I told him about Leanne's visit. He had not known about the Matlings being her parents. He found Leanne's version of the origin of the box easy to believe, but he was fond of Leanne and a little gullible when his heart was involved. He wanted to go straight over to her flat to see her, but I needed him to help me with the influx of clients who came to the Vintage for coffee and cake. I don't know how they had found out Ghita had begun to bake again, but I suspected Roz of being the source of that piece of news. Her ability to spread a rumour often had an upside. I also had a visit from Joe Brennan to buy the cloisonné box. I had put it aside after I saw him gazing at it and I had guessed right about his interest. His mother's birthday turned out to be the reason for his purchase.

Later that afternoon, I sold the early Habitat shelves we had found at the Shoreham boot sale to a woman who told me she had the same ones at home and had searched far and wide for another set to put with them. I offered to deliver them to her house, and she left me her address on a piece of paper. Once the mini-rush had subsided, Mouse asked me if he could leave. I could tell he would go straight to comfort Leanne, and I warned him to be careful not to talk about the investigation with her, just in case she was more involved than she seemed. We had had access to information which had not been released to the general public and could alert the culprit to our progress in the case. Mouse left in a huff after that, but I knew he would think about what I had said and come round eventually. He was still a teenager, and it showed.

I shut the shop early and headed for the side street to the promenade. I caught a glance of Kieron sitting at one of the tables in Surfusion, his head lowered into his hands. His posture spoke of capitulation. I decided to talk to him about the investigation. I could raise his spirits by imparting some of the information I had without giving other things away. He sprang up as if electrocuted when I tapped on the window. He shook his head at me, but I persisted, mouthing 'I have news' at him. He pulled his brows together to look ferocious, but I would not budge. He didn't scare me and he needed my help no matter how rude he had been in the past.

'What do you want?' he said, opening the door a few inches.

'And a very good evening to you too,' I said, pushing past him. 'Aren't you going to offer me a glass of wine?'

'Aren't you afraid I'll poison you too?' he said.

'Not really. Mine's a large red.'

He sighed, as if put upon, and took a bottle off the shelf, pouring us both a full glass of Pinot Noir.

'Cheers,' I said.

'I don't know what you're so happy about,' he said. 'All our high-end clients would have gone to your shop after a few glasses of wine at lunch, and spent a fortune. Now they're all gone, like migrating birds, never to return.'

He took a big gulp of wine. I wondered if I should inform him that migrating birds always came back to the same place, but he probably knew that already. I could smell sweat and drink emanating from him and I knew it wasn't his first drink of the day. For somebody so picky about his appearance, Kieron's appearance had fallen far from his pedestal of good taste and hygiene. The front of his t-shirt had a dried in stain which might have been coffee. His normally manicured nails were bitten to the quick. Even his usually immaculate eyebrows, plucked no doubt by Rohan, were unkempt and bushy. I don't believe in kicking a man when he's down, but he had secrets which were key to the investigation.

'You asked me about the autopsy results before. Do you still want to know what they are?'

His head snapped up.

'Of course I do.'

'Would it interest you to know that the stomach contents of the man who died contained a large dose of laxatives?'

I thought he might faint. He grasped the edge of the table and forced out a few words.

'Did it kill him?'

'No. But it seems to me you know how it got in there.'

He swallowed.

'I heard them,' he said. 'Rohan and Ghita. Talking about the baby. They didn't even ask me what I thought about it. How could he keep such a massive thing from me? I blame her. We were happy until she started interfering in our relationship.'

'Ghita? But she's kind and gentle and she loves you both. She wouldn't do anything to hurt you. Rohan should have told you about their plans, but they hadn't done anything about it yet. He was waiting for the restaurant to open first.'

His eyes opened wide.

'You knew? I can't believe it. Why didn't anyone tell me? I'm the important one around here.'

'Maybe they knew how you would react? Did you put the laxative in the moules?'

'Yes, but it was for Ghita. She wasn't supposed to give it to Black. I tried to stop her, but it was too late. And then the review came in and the sky fell in. I completely lost it. I haven't recovered to tell you the truth. But why did Black die?'

'Firstly, it wasn't Black, but an imposter. We think someone else sent him to sabotage your opening night.'

'An imposter. But what about the review?'

'We think that may be fake too. Someone may have hacked into Black's blog.'

'But why did he die? Did we kill him?'

'Anaphylactic shock. There were peanuts in the prawn ceviche.'

'Peanuts? But that's impossible. We don't have peanuts in our kitchen. How on earth did they get into the ceviche?'

'It's a long story, not one I can tell you yet, but trust me, it has nothing to do with your cooking.'

Kieron took another big swig of his wine and wiped his mouth with the back of his hand. He sat blinking for a few seconds as he took in this new information, then he frowned.

'Have you got the review on your phone?' he said. 'I haven't read it again since that terrible night.'

'I took a screenshot.'

I passed him my phone, and he read the review again, grimacing and shaking his head. Then he stopped still. He pointed at the screen.

'Oh my goodness. I should have noticed before, but I was suffering from shock.'

'Noticed what?' I said.

'The scallops. He says they were vile tasting and half rotten.'

'So?'

'Ed couldn't find any scallops for us. We had to make last-minute changes to the menu. We replaced the scallops with king prawns.'

'Oh! I remember now. Mouse had to help you redo the menus.'

'Whoever wrote the review, it wasn't the person who came to Surfusion. Only a few people got the original menu with the scallop dish on it. Rohan knows who they are.'

'Can you ask him to send me a list? We need to find out who sent that review.'

'But what have they got to do with the imposter's death?'

'I don't know, but it's beginning to look like the perfect storm as far as sabotaging your restaurant goes.'

'Please don't stop investigating. You can't imagine the stress I'm under. My mother has achieved Olympic standard at emotional blackmail and it's sucking my soul out.'

'You're a dutiful son. She should be proud of you.'

'She doesn't show it.'

'Mothers can be light on praise and heavy on blackmail. It's their revenge for all the worry of your early years. I'm sure she loves you.'

He shrugged.

'She did, before I came out. Now I'm not sure. Look, I know I haven't been very polite to you in the past, and I'm sorry, but Rohan and I put blood and sweat into this venture, and he's my soulmate. It can't fail, or we might be finished. I can't lose him.'

His lower lip quivered and almost broke my heart for him.

'I'm not in the habit of giving up,' I said. 'Leave it with me,'

Chapter 25

I didn't have to wait long for Rohan to text me a list of the people who had received a copy of the original menu. It dropped into my message folder as I arrived home at the Grotty Hovel. I gave a fist pump as realised what it was and forwarded it to Mouse.

'What's this?' he said.

'It's a list of people who saw the menu before Kieron removed the scallop dish. Whoever wrote the review on Leonard Black's site didn't realise the scallops had been replaced with a ceviche.'

Mouse's eyes widened.

'I can't believe we didn't spot that before. Give me a minute to google everyone and see if any name pops out.'

I went to the kitchen and took a bottle of wine out of the cupboard before replacing it again. I needed to be sharp. Instead, I made myself a cup of tea and went to sit with Mouse. His fingers flew over the keyboard as he tutted and clicked to himself.

'I think we can discount Kieron's mother,' I said. 'She has a motive, as she wants him to abandon Seacastle and come home to live with her, but Kieron told me she doesn't have access to a computer.'

'She doesn't even have a Facebook account,' said Mouse. 'Even you've got one of these.'

I forgave the dig at my former status as a confirmed Luddite. My life had changed forever since the night Mouse broke into the Grotty Hovel and took over my spare bedroom. My adult life could be divided into two halves; B.M (Before Mouse) when I existed in the fug of clinical depression with no internet access or smart phone, and A.M (After Mouse). Mouse had introduced me to the internet and smartphones, and made me buy a new laptop. He dragged me into the daylight of the twenty-first century and enabled me to reconnect with all my old friends from my days working on 'Uncovering the Truth'. It reawakened my interest in investigative journalism and sleuthing.

B.M was not an era of time I remembered with fondness. My marriage to George had broken down when he met a younger clone of me without my medical problems. I had found myself kicked out of the marital home, struggling to earn enough to survive. A.M gave me Mouse and Harry, and brought me back together with my sister Helen. I got my spark back too.

Mouse had a point about Facebook. Many of my friends were my age and older, and most of them had Facebook accounts. Mouse's generation had fled in horror from the platform as their mothers and aunts had insisted on 'friending' them and commented on their posts. They now lurked on the fringes of TikTok and Snapchat and other undiscovered countries ready to flee again if anyone older than twenty-five appeared on their feeds.

'Oh my days,' said Mouse. 'I recognise this name. Krish Patel. He's one of the guys who belongs to my hacking group, not that I do that anymore,' he added, too hastily I thought.

'I wasn't born yesterday, as you so often point out,' I said. 'I'm well aware of your dubious online activities. Does this man have any links to our investigation?'

'He's Rohan's younger brother.'

'Now that sounds promising. Would he have the skills to hack into Leonard Black's blog site?'

'I should think so. It had single password access until recently. Any idiot could have…'

He trailed off as I arched an eyebrow.

'Did you?' I asked.

He shrugged.

'Of course I did. You told me to find out who Leonard Black was, remember? I thought I might find out from the blog site, but we got sidetracked with other clues.'

'Could you get back into the site now?'

'I'm not sure. He's upped security since the review was posted. But I could try.'

'And Rohan's brother?'

'What about him?'

'Can we track him down?'

'Sure, but why would he want to sabotage Surfusion?'

'He disapproves of Rohan's lifestyle choices. Maybe he thought Rohan and Kieron would break up if the restaurant closed down.'

Mouse's face made me snort.

'You think Kieron counts as a lifestyle choice?'

'Well, not specifically, although I'm not convinced that I approve of Kieron myself most of the time.'

'Oh. You mean Rohan being gay. That's not a choice though, is it?'

'Some people think it is. Rohan told me his brother tried to blackmail him into getting married and living a normal life.'

'But being gay is normal, isn't it? Is that why Rohan dated Ghita?'

'I think that was his mother's idea. She didn't expect them to have a genuine marriage, just turn up together for family occasions together, and so on.'

He rubbed his nose.

'I'm not sure I want to adult. It's far too complicated.'

'I know what you mean. I'm not sure how Rohan will feel about us talking to his brother under these circumstances. Is there any way you can set up a meeting and get some information from him? Does he trust you?'

'Probably. Leave it with me. And I'll see if one of the guys can find out what Leonard Black's real name is too. It might cost us, though.'

'Let's try our way first. If we can't find him, we can ask your friends for help. Just don't tell George what we're doing or he'll arrest us both.'

'I'm going to university to study hacking for a living. The police are paying. I don't know why this is any different.'

'Neither do I. Let's see if he will speak to us.'

153

Chapter 26

George messaged me the next morning asking me to come down to the station. He rarely talked to me at his place of work, so I assumed our parallel investigations were converging at last. My heart rate increased as I abandoned the shop and strode down the High Street. Grace saw me passing and waved at me to stop, but I didn't have time to fill her in on my mission. I increased my pace and arrived at the station steps, panting with exertion. I was almost knocked over by the Matlings leaving through the station doors, their faces twinned in thunder and resentment. Keith Matling recognised me and lunged at me, missing me by inches.

'I should have guessed,' he said. 'Who do you think you are? Miss Marple? You've got some cheek involving us in this farce.'

'Imagine blaming that man's death on our little girl,' said his wife. 'You interfering busybody. No wonder he divorced you.'

I watched the Matlings stomp away. I presumed they would go straight to Leanne's flat and berate her for 'snitching on them'. I felt sorry for her and in a small way for them too. As much as I disliked them both, the idea of them sabotaging the Surfusion seemed farfetched to me. Surfusion's account was small beer to them and they were more likely to take it out on Ed Murray. I pitied Leanne for having such aggressive parents. No wonder she had moved out with her sister as soon as they could afford it.

I pushed open the station doors and found Sally Wright guarding the reception desk. I rolled my eyes at her and she grinned in sympathy.

'They weren't happy to be called in for an interview,' she said. 'I think they blamed you.'

'I'm sure they did,' I said. 'Can I go through and see George?'

'He's waiting for you in interview room one with Flo. Shall I get you a cuppa?'

'Oh, yes, please. I'm gasping.'

I walked through the office to the interview room, giving a wave to George's team, most of whom I still recognised. My occasional contributions to their investigations had won me their respect since George and I had parted. I wondered what they made of his relationship with my sister Helen. Grist to the mill, no doubt. Even I had to admit it was a little weird in the beginning. I took off my shoes at the door of the interview room to ground myself against the electric shocks I got from the artificial fibre carpet in there. George hated when I did that. He frowned at me, but for once he didn't comment. Flo stood up and gave me a hug. She wore a cheesecloth top the size of a tablecloth. It was like being hugged by a cheerful picnic. I love Flo.

'Did you bump into the Matlings?' she asked with a wicked smile.

'Keith tried to have a close encounter, but I swerved him.'

'Did he touch you?' said George. 'I'd be more than happy to charge him with assault. Aggressive sod!'

'No need,' I said. 'I'd be more worried about Leanne to tell you the truth. Have you got any news for me?'

'The analysis found peanut powder residue in the Matling's box, so it's definitely the source of the contamination.'

'That's fantastic. Well, not fantastic. You know what I mean.'

George pursed his lips, and I shut up again.

'We have analysed the fingerprints lifted from the Matling's prawn box,' said Flo. 'As expected, Leanne's fingerprints feature prominently, but there's a second set on there.'

'Anyone we know?' I asked.

'Not exactly, but one of the prints matches the one we found on the chip inside the burner phone,' said George.

I clapped my hands together. Finally, a link between two elements in this labyrinthine investigation.

'The same person who put the chip into the burner phone must have hired Alan Miller and organised the delivery of the contaminated prawns to Surfusion.'

'But did they also post the horrible review on Leonard Black's blog?' asked Flo.

'I don't think so,' I said. 'I spoke to Kieron yesterday, and we realised that whoever wrote the review must have received a copy of the original menu for opening night.'

'The original menu? Did it change?' said George.

'Yes. Ed Murray couldn't source any fresh scallops, so they had to put prawn ceviche on the menu instead. The people who received the menu had strict instructions not to show it to anyone else, and they wouldn't have been aware of the change.'

'That means only one of them could have written the review. Do you have a list of names?'

I smirked and took out my phone.

'Here is one I made earlier,' I said, forwarding it to him.

George pressed the intercom.

'Sally, can you get PC Brennan in here, please?'

He rubbed his hands together.

'Now we're motoring. I'll get Joe to take their fingerprints for elimination purposes. We'll soon know whose prints are on the box.'

'It's probably not worth bothering with some of them. Kieron's mother is an invalid and doesn't have internet access.'

'We can't assume anything,' said George. 'Isn't she the old woman who is constantly pretending to be dying to get him to visit her?'

'Well, yes, but I hardly think—'

George snorted.

'That's your problem, Tan. You hardly think. She could have planned the whole thing from her bed. She has enough motive.'

I bristled. Sometimes I wanted to punch George squarely on the nose. Joe Brennan put his head around the door.

'You wanted to see me, boss?'

'Yes. Can you get fingerprints from all the people on a list I'm about to forward to you? You'll need to compare the prints with the ones already in the database from the mobile phone chip and the Matling's box.'

'Right away. Can I take PC Strong with me? She's good at putting people at their ease. It'll speed up the process.'

'Okay. If anyone lives nearby, call them in to the station and put their prints directly into the system using the Livescan. Once you've got them covered, see if you can get prints from people who live further away. You may be able to liaise with some of the other forces to do that.'

'Did you learn anything else from Kieron?' said Flo.

I could feel myself colouring under her gaze.

'Um, well, to tell you the truth, I did. I found out why our victim had a large dose of laxatives in his stomach.'

'Laxatives?' said George. 'Are they dangerous?'

'Not at all,' said Flo. 'It was just weird.'

'Kieron confessed he dropped some into Miller's bowl by accident and Ghita took it out to the table before he could stop her.'

'Would it have contributed to his death?' asked George.

'Absolutely not,' said Flo. 'The anaphylactic shock combined with his asthma made his death inevitable.'

'Well, that's one less thing to worry about,' said George.

'I'll put it in the file,' said Flo. 'Just in case. Thanks for telling me.'

'Oh, no problem. He had been panicking about it. I'll set him straight.'

'Honestly, this case is so complicated, it's doing my head in,' said George. 'We don't even know if there is a murderer involved yet.'

'It's more likely to be a case of sabotage gone horribly wrong,' I said. 'But we haven't chased down all the leads yet.'

'Well, leave the police work to us,' said George. 'But if you hear anything pertinent to the investigation, I'd be glad if you kept us informed. This entire episode is unfathomable.'

'It's hard for Rohan and Kieron too. Their livelihoods are at stake.'

'Do you think they'll ever open Surfusion again?' asked Flo.

'It's in the lap of the gods,' I said. 'Even if they open it, the customers may not return.'

Flo followed me out into the reception of the police station and we stood on the steps in the sun for a moment.

'Why did Kieron dose the food with laxatives?' said Flo. 'Are you sure it had nothing to do with the whole fiasco?'

'Pretty sure. He meant to give them to Ghita and there was a mix-up.'

'Ghita? What did she do?'

'Kieron overheard Rohan discussing the possibility of having a baby with her. He's a hothead and insanely jealous where Rohan is concerned. He wanted to get her back.'

'Oh, that explains it. Have they talked about it yet?'

'I don't think so. I found Kieron brooding yesterday. Rohan hasn't come back from his parents' house yet and Ghita is staying well away from the Surfusion for now.'

'What a mess.'

'And we still don't know why poor Alan Miller died.'

'We're getting closer though, aren't we?'

'I think so. I have a couple of leads I haven't followed up yet.'

'Does George know?'

'After his rudeness today, I think I'll check them out myself first, just to be sure he won't dismiss them as hardly thinking again.'

'He doesn't mean it. He's just frustrated. This case has driven him bonkers.'

'Me too. Nothing fits.'

'Let's hope Joe Brennan comes up trumps,' said Flo. 'You'll tell me if you turn something up?'

'I promise.'

Chapter 27

I walked back along the High Street to Second Home. Nearly every shop had a sale on, but I didn't feel in the slightest bit tempted. I've always been good at cutting my coat according to my cloth and I had been saving money to help Mouse pay his university expenses. The police grant paid his fees, but he had to fend for himself as far as living expenses were concerned. I hoped George would also contribute, but I wasn't holding my breath.

Mouse greeted me cheerfully as I entered, waving a five-pound note in the air with a flourish.

'I sold a lampshade. We're rich,' he said. 'Well, I can afford to buy milk for the coffee anyway.'

'Excellent news. Pop out and get it now while there's a lull.'

He didn't point out that the entire week had been a lull, except for fans of Ghita's cakes who had already eaten their way through three of them. While he went to the Co-Op, I took out my notebook and wrote down everything I could remember about the meeting with George and Flo. The news about the fingerprints felt like a breakthrough. I doubted any of the people who had received the original menu were responsible for the rest of the events, except for Rohan's brother. He had crept on to my list of suspects with his hacking skills. Mouse needed to set up a meeting as soon as possible. We had made progress at last. When I finished writing the notes,

I scrolled mindlessly through my phone while I waited for a customer.

The doorbell clanged, and I looked up to see Mouse come in. His brow furrowed. He put the milk on the counter and took his mobile phone out of his pocket.

'I just received this text from Leanne,' he said. 'I thought you already talked to her about the box. I'm a little worried.'

I took the phone from him and read the message. *I've remembered something important about what happened at Surfusion. It might be dangerous. I've got to talk to you. Will you be in the shop later?*

'Dangerous? I don't understand. To whom?'

'I don't know. I'll tell her to come over as soon as she can.'

'Should we pick her up?'

'She already told me her parents are going to visit her there shortly.'

'Ah, perhaps not right now, then. Don't worry. As soon as she gets back in touch, we can drive over and get her.'

'Okay.'

Soon local office workers started arriving with their sandwiches and Tupperware boxes of salad for lunch at the Vintage. I had never discouraged them from eating their own food upstairs. As long as they bought a coffee, I was glad of their custom. Mouse served them all with a smile despite his preoccupation. Leanne's text had made us both worry. What on earth could she mean by dangerous? Had she forgotten, or neglected, to tell me something which now made her feel unsafe? I hoped nobody would linger long after their lunch. We needed to collect Leanne as soon as possible and take her to the police station for safety.

By the time the last customers left, I had worked myself into a panic. I shouted up the stairs at Mouse to leave the washing up for later and to come with me in the car to collect Leanne. The doorbell rang, and I turned to tell the person entering that unfortunately we were closing. To my surprise, Leanne's mother came in. I stepped backwards, colliding with the counter in my haste.

'What do you want?' I said. 'I'll call the police if you don't leave.'

Her face creased with anguish.

'It's my Leanne,' she said. 'She's gone.'

Mouse came running down the stairs.

'Mrs Matling? What's happened?'

'Leanne has disappeared.'

'Wasn't she supposed to meet you earlier?'

'We went to her flat to meet her, but she didn't answer the door, so we let ourselves in.'

'You have a key?'

'Yes, she gave it to me in case of emergencies, but I'm not supposed to use it. We searched the place, but Leanne had gone and her handbag had been emptied out onto the table.'

'Was it a robbery?' I asked.

'Her wallet was lying there untouched.'

'Have you tried texting her?' said Mouse.

'I think her phone is switched off.'

'Is there any reason she might have run away?' I asked.

'I don't know, but she told me she recognised someone in the street, a taxi driver, I think, who had something to do with that restaurant where she worked. I'm not sure what she meant. She thought he might be following her.'

'She can't have gone far, but I suggest you tell the police just in case.'

'The police? But they think we have something to do with the death at Surfusion. What if they think we harmed our daughter?'

'That isn't what they told me. George is my ex-husband, and I promise you, he is a serious copper. He'll find Leanne.'

'We can help,' said Mouse. 'I've met lots of her friends. Let me find out if she is staying with any of them.'

'What about her sister?' I said.

Mrs Matling shook her head.

'She won't speak to me. Not since she left home. She'll blame me for this too.'

'She might speak to us, though. Why don't you let me try? I know we didn't get off to the best start, but my son is fond of your daughter and that's good enough for me.'

'My name's Maeve,' she said. 'Maeve Matling.'

'And I'm Tanya. Don't worry, Maeve. I've been sleuthing for a few years now, and I'm pretty successful. Mouse and I will do our best to find her, but please tell DI Carter about this too.'

'Okay. I'll go right there.'

'Here's my card. Can you text me so I can save your contact details?'

'Right away. Thank you.'

After she had left, I collected my things and shut the shop. Mouse and I trotted to the Mini and set out for the building where Leanne lived with her sister, Nieve. My heart thundered as I tried to stay within the speed limit. Mouse sat pale and silent in the passenger seat, texting Leanne from his phone.

Leanne lived out near the large supermarket in the top flat of a divided terraced house. Her sister Nieve answered the doorbell and buzzed the intercom for us to enter. We climbed the narrow staircase into their tiny flat.

Mouse had already told me that Leanne slept in the bedroom and her sister in the sitting room, and I was expecting chaos. Instead, I was surprised by the neatness of the flat and the bunch of fresh flowers on the small table in the kitchen corner.

Nieve looked so like Leanne that I thought for an instant that Leanne had returned. She kissed Mouse and stood awkwardly, wondering like me how we should introduce ourselves.

'I'm Tanya, Mouse's mother,' I said. 'Can you tell us what happened?'

'I'm not really sure. I was about to leave because our parents were coming to see Leanne. We, um, don't speak these days. Anyway, Leanne answered the intercom and when she saw who was downstairs, she turned pale and ran out of the flat. I think she exited by the fire escape. When I checked the intercom screen to speak to him, whoever it was had already gone.'

'Did she say anything to you?' said Mouse.

'Oh no, it's him again. How did he find me? Tell him you haven't seen me. That's all she said before taking off. She took nothing with her except for her phone.'

'Do you think she might come back?'

'I presume so. She doesn't have anywhere else to go.'

'Can you tell her we need to speak to her? Urgently. We need to know where she saw this man before. He may be the key to a murder investigation.'

'Murder? No wonder she ran away.'

'It's not officially murder yet, but she's right to be frightened. If she comes back, tell her she can stay with us until it's safe.'

After we left the flat, Mouse refused to get into the car and said he would go around some of their usual haunts to see if Leanne had gone there to hide. I told him not to worry, that we would find her in time. I'm not sure he believed me, as I had trouble convincing myself.

Leanne's disappearance depressed me more than I expected. I felt as if I would never unravel the mystery of what happened that night at Surfusion. Mouse did not come home for supper, but stayed out in the hope she might turn up. If I had been affected this way, I couldn't imagine how poor Rohan and Kieron were coping. When Harry noticed how droopy I looked, he made me some soft-boiled eggs and buttered toast to boost my morale. Even one of my favourite foods could not lure me out of the doldrums as I struggled with my mood.

Despite my protests that I couldn't face any more sleuthing, Harry cleaned off the whiteboard and wrote down what we already knew. The laxatives had turned out to be a red herring. The awful review probably had nothing to do with the incident at Surfusion, but we had a firm lead to the perpetrator which we needed to follow up asap. The key pieces of evidence were the Matling's box of prawns and the burner phone. These items were linked by an identical fingerprint whose owner we needed to trace.

'How did Miller get to the Surfusion from London?'

'Didn't Miller's girlfriend Susanne tell us he took the train to Seacastle?'

'I think so. I can check my notes.'

'But how did he get to the restaurant? Somebody must have given him a lift.'

'A taxi driver, presumably?' I said.

'But the police already canvassed the taxi drivers and nobody remembered taking Miller to the restaurant.'

'You'd think he would have stood out in his flashy disguise. It seems weird nobody noticed him arriving.'

'But maybe nobody asked them,' said Harry.

'What do you mean?'

'Well, in the beginning, the police assumed Miller had died by misadventure or, at a stretch, of food poisoning. When the taxi drivers denied bringing him to Surfusion, they didn't continue to question people about how he got there.'

'So?'

'Why don't we contact the people sitting at the window tables and ask them if they saw anything? The people who live in the street opposite Surfusion might also have seen something. Miller's bizarre outfit may have stuck in their minds.'

'That's a great idea. You're a genius. And we also need to talk to Rohan's brother about the review.'

'There you go. The investigation isn't dead. It's just getting going.'

Chapter 28

The next morning, I leapt out of bed, almost doing myself permanent damage when I trod on a small piece of mouse Hades had left on the bedroom floor and I slid into the wardrobe. Swearing, I picked myself up and headed for the shower. When he stopped laughing, Harry made us some breakfast. Mouse stumbled down the stairs when the smell of sausages penetrated his slumber. I couldn't resist mussing his rebellious black curls, provoking a grunt of protest, but not so strong that I stopped.

'Did you have any luck finding Leanne last night?' I asked.

'No, but her sister Nieve texted me to say they had been in contact and to wait for Leanne to speak when she is ready.'

'At least she's okay,' I said. 'But that's pretty frustrating. She knows something that may be key to the investigation.'

'What's all that stuff on the whiteboard?'

'Harry and I were brainstorming last night. We're going to talk to the locals to see if they spotted Alan Miller's arrival at Surfusion. They may have seen the man who dropped him off.'

'That's a great idea.'

'Also, we need you to set up a meeting with Rohan's brother, Krish Patel. Do you think he'll come to the Vintage?'

'He might be more likely to come to the Shanty. He likes a drink, and it's a more neutral venue. I'll contact him and ask him to come this evening.'

Mouse tapped away on his phone for about five minutes and finally raised his head.

'He'll meet us there tonight at six-thirty.'

'Wow, quick work. That's great, thanks.'

'I hope he's in a cooperative mood. The review he wrote left little room for doubt about his intent,' said Harry.

'That's why you're coming too,' I said.

After breakfast we headed for Surfusion and Second Home, dropping some crusts in the wind shelter in case Herbert should be hungry. The sea had retreated almost to its fullest extent and sheets of bright green algae covered the sand between the rock pools. The wind turbines stood out against the blue sky bordering the new marine protected area where sea life regrew and thrived. I liked to imagine the small fry playing among the giant kelp fronds. Harry reached for my hand and I felt his large warm one envelop mine. As always, it gave me teenage thrills to walk hand in hand with him. He made me feel giddy, but safe in a way I had never experienced before.

'You look in love,' said Mouse. 'I'm jealous.'

'You're included in the circle. You can hold my other hand if you want to.'

'No way! What if one of my friends saw me?'

Harry chuckled.

'You can't have your cake and eat it too,' he said.

'Unless you work in Second Home,' I said, handing Mouse the keys.

'Does that mean I can have a slice?'

'You've just had breakfast.'

'I'm a growing boy.'

We parted company at the top of King Street and Mouse turned right to Second home while we turned left to Surfusion.

'Where do we start?' said Harry.

'We can get the customers' names from Rohan if we don't have any luck from the neighbours. Let's try the shops on either side of the restaurant.'

It soon became apparent that the shops would not yield up any information as they were all closed by the time Surfusion had opened its door on the night of the inauguration. We tried the doorbell of the flat above the restaurant and we were buzzed in by a tiny raisin of a man whose false teeth had a life of their own. I tried not to stare at them as they slid around on his jaws. He rubbed his chin when asked about the opening.

'Oh yes, I was here that night. Mind you, I'm as deaf as a post, so I heard nothing. Wasn't someone shot?'

'Gosh, no. Nothing like that. We're trying to trace somebody who came to the opening. He wore flamboyant clothes and had an enormous hat on his head.'

'I didn't see anyone in particular. I wasn't looking, you see. My favourite program had just started on television and I have to read the sub-titles if I want to follow it.'

'Thank you for your help. I'm sorry to bother you.'

'Oh, no bother. You're in the wrong place if you want information, though. You need to visit the Gestapo over there in number forty-seven. Didn't you see the curtains twitching as you arrived? She misses nothing. She's even worse since she got that phone of hers.'

'Does she have a name?' said Harry.

'Gladys Fitch. Rhymes with—'

'Thank you. We'll take it from here,' I said, cutting him off.

We descended to the street and peered up above the doorway of number forty-seven. Sure enough, a spotless lace curtain fell back into place as we looked upwards. Harry elbowed me.

'Did you see?' he said.

'I did.'

We rang the doorbell and a querulous voice answered.

'Are you the people who were visiting across the street?' it said.

'That's us,' I said. 'Are you Gladys Fitch?'

'Who's asking?'

'I'm Tanya Bowe, a private investigator and—'

The door clicked open before I could finish.

We mounted the stairs to find Mrs Fitch waiting at her door.

'Come in,' she said. 'I'm a private investigator too, in my own way.'

'It's an honour to meet you. This is Harry Fletch, my associate.'

'Associate? I saw you holding hands. He's your boyfriend.'

'I see we can't fool you,' I said. 'Maybe you can help us.'

'What do you want?'

'The man who lives opposite told us you run the local neighbourhood watch.'

'Did he now? He's an idiot. I just keep an eye on things.'

'Were you here the night the Surfusion opened?'

'I'm always here.'

'Did you watch the people arriving for dinner?'

She smirked.

'I did. I watched them all leave too, when that man died.'

'I'm sure you noticed an odd-looking man in a long cloak going inside.'

'He had a wig on too. I could see it from here.'

'Did you see how he got here?'

She put her head on one side and blinked a couple of times. I could almost imagine her running a Rolodex in her head.

'He came as a passenger in a car.'

'So not a taxi?'

'It looked like a private car.'

'How did you figure that out?'

'The man in the cloak sat in the front seat and he didn't pay the driver.'

'Did you see the driver?'

'Not really. He had dark hair, but I couldn't see his face. The driver's side window was open, and he had a tattoo on his forearm.'

'I'm guessing you didn't make a note of the registration number?' said Harry.

'You guessed right, but I took a photograph of him entering the restaurant in case he was famous. I think the car is also in the photo.'

Somehow, I managed not to leap in the air with excitement. As casually as I could, I asked, 'do you still have the photograph?'

Gladys Fitch stood up and hobbled across the sitting room. She reached for her phone, which sat on the windowsill and scrolled through it, tutting and shaking her head.

'Oh, gosh, where is it? I hope I didn't delete it. Um, okay, here are some people arriving. What a tarty dress that woman is wearing! Honestly. Oh, no, wait, um, yes, here it is.'

She shoved the screen in my face. I took it from her and gazed at it. I could see Alan Miller, frozen in time, opening the door of the restaurant. His wig looked even more bizarre from above. The roof of the car was obscured by the reflection from the streetlamps, but, sure enough, I could see a tattooed arm leaning on the edge of the open window.

'This is fantastic. It will be a big help in the investigation into the unexplained death at Surfusion. Can you please send this to me, if I give my number to you?'

'Of course.'

I wrote down my number and she put it into her phone. My mobile phone pinged almost immediately.

'Thank you so much.'

'Oh, don't thank me, dear. I haven't got anything better to do. People call me a nosy parker, because I watch them out of my window, but I'm just interested in what's going on. My world has shrunk to what I can see in the street below my flat.'

'Would you like to know how we get on?' said Harry.

Her face lit up.

'Really? I'd be so excited to find out. Nothing interesting ever happens to me anymore.'

'We'll be in touch then,' I said. 'And if you remember anything else, please send me a text and I'll come and chat again.'

Her face fell.

'There is something. I should tell you now, but I'm worried you won't come back.'

'Can you walk fifty yards?' I said.

'Just about.'

'Well, in that case, you can come and ask for me at my shop, Second Home.'

'I know it. It's got all that interesting bric-a-brac.'

'That's right. I'll stand you a hot beverage too.'

'Thank you. Well, I'm pretty sure I've seen that car before.'

'The car that brought the man in the cloak to the restaurant?'

'Yes, I can't be sure when, but I saw it lurking in the street in the days around the opening. I may have made a note somewhere. I'll have to look.'

She gestured hopelessly at the piles of newspapers and magazines and books stacked all around the flat.

'I make notes on the margins of the newspaper while I'm reading it and looking out of the window at the same time. It's not very scientific, I'm afraid.'

'We can wait. It would be marvellous if you could give us a day when you saw it.'

'Oh, if I find my notes, I'll be able to give you a time as well.'

Chapter 29

We made the short walk back to Second Home and made ourselves a coffee. Our meeting with Gladys Fitch had been a revelation. She had a point about people's prejudices about old women and net curtains. I must admit I had a bias against nosy parkers myself. How ironic considering I was the biggest one in town! I forwarded the photograph she had taken to George, and to Mouse who got to work trying to enhance the tattoo on the driver's arm. I texted George, suggesting he send a PC to interview Gladys, knowing how thrilled she would be to contribute to the investigation.

When we had finished our coffee, Harry left to deliver some furniture for Grace and Max while I sat in the shop twiddling my thumbs. I could hardly wait for six-thirty and the meeting with Krish Patel at the Shanty. To my surprise, Rohan and Kieron turned up for a chat. They both had bags under their eyes and were grey with exhaustion. I got the impression they had fought themselves to a standstill. I made them sit down in the window seat and waited for one of them to say something. Finally, Rohan gesticulated at Kieron.

'He told me about the laxative,' he said. 'I can't believe it.'

'It was a little over the top, but I can understand his reaction. I warned you that you ought to tell him about your discussions with Ghita.'

'I know it's my fault. I wanted to tell Kieron what we were thinking, but we hadn't decided yet, and he was so stressed,' said Rohan. 'I would never have gone ahead without involving him in every minute.'

'I know. I'm just a jealous idiot. And Ghita has been so wonderful with us. We need her in our lives.'

'Is it true the laxative didn't hurt that poor man?' asked Rohan.

'Yes, Flo says it didn't have time to act. The man died of anaphylactic shock.'

'So we killed him anyway?'

'No. But somebody did. Can I speak frankly? I've got all sorts of information we didn't have before, but it's confidential.'

They looked at each other, and Rohan linked his little finger through Kieron's. Kieron swallowed and his big blue eyes filled with tears.

'Pinky promise,' he said.

Rohan nodded. They sat opposite me with the fingers interlinked. It seemed like neither of them wanted to let go. I fought the urge to dissolve in a sobbing heap.

'Okay then. George and I have done some investigating. As I already told Kieron, the man who died was not a food critic. Someone is trying to sabotage your restaurant. Harry and I talked to a neighbour who saw Alan Miller arrive. She took a photograph of him getting out of the car. It's not very good I'm afraid, but you can see a man driving who had a tattoo on his arm.'

'Can you see the design?' said Rohan.

'Not yet, but Mouse is going to work on it with his photo enhancing software. Hopefully, we can get some idea about what it is.'

'I'd like to see it when it's ready,' said Kieron, who had gone pale.

'Is there something you've remembered?' said Rohan, but Kieron just shook his head.

'Everyone's got a tattoo these days,' he said.

'There's another piece of news. I'm afraid it might be upsetting for you Rohan,' I said.

He shrugged.

'More upsetting than the last few weeks? I doubt it.'

'I'm not one hundred per cent sure yet, but I think I know who hacked Leonard Black's site and posted the review.'

'Go on.'

'Kieron sent us a list of the people who received the original menu for opening night. They are the only people who knew about the scallop dish. One of them was your brother.'

Rohan bit his lip and hung his head.

'And?' he said.

'Mouse says he's a well-known hacker who belongs to some of their groups. He is the only one on the list with the skills to hack Black's blog.'

'Are you saying he wrote the review?'

'We're going to meet him later. I expect him to confirm it.'

'Oh no! I'm so sorry, Kieron. I didn't have any idea he was capable of anything like this.'

'It's not your fault. I put the laxatives in the food. Someone else spiked the prawns and sent a prankster. Our opening night was doomed to failure.'

'How can we come back from this?' said Rohan. 'Maybe we should close permanently? Everyone will associate our restaurant with murder.'

My heart broke for them. Maybe Rohan was right. Maybe there was no way back. But then I had a strong feeling of déjà vu and the pink shiny face of Tim Boulting, manager of the Tarton Manor House hotel, loomed into my mind's eye.

'Murder weekends,' I said.

Rohan and Kieron stared at me as if I had said something blasphemous or horrendous.

'I beg your pardon?' said Kieron.

'Oh, no, I mean, ignore me. I just remembered something unrelated. I apologise.'

'Well, we're all a little distraught,' said Rohan, pursing his lips.

I felt like laughing, but I couldn't tell them why my mood had lifted so much. Might I have the solution for the relaunch? I didn't dare hope. I refocused.

'Look, I'm going to talk to your brother about the review and I'm going to come down heavy on him. Perhaps threaten him with prison. Not that I have the right to arrest him, but he doesn't know that. He'll be left feeling he caused the death of Alan Miller. It's a little mean, but writing the review does not qualify as civilised behaviour either. It might be a good time to mend your fences. Get him to talk to you about things. Perhaps introduce him to Kieron? What do you think?'

'Do you think he'd listen?' said Rohan.

'I don't know. He's your brother. Didn't he love you once?'

'We were like twins. Until he found out. Then… Well, you can see how he feels.'

'I'm meeting him at six-thirty at the Shanty. If you come there about fifteen minutes later, you may get an opening with him. It's worth a try.'

'Gone on, darling. I'll come with you. How can he resist my charms?' said Kieron.

'With great ease,' said Rohan. 'But we have to try. Maybe he'll be ready to talk.'

'I expect he already knows what happened on opening night,' I said. 'All I have to do is persuade him he's partially responsible, if he doesn't think so already…'

'I'll be there,' said Rohan. 'I've got to go home and pick something up first.'

They left arm in arm, shaken, but less bowed. I hoped they had turned a corner. I waited until they had left the shop and then I scrolled through my phone, looking for Lydia Sheldon's phone number. She was the owner of the Tarton Manor House where Tim Boulting worked. I texted her a message asking her if she could meet me, crossing my fingers that she wouldn't turn down my idea flat.

Harry turned up at six o'clock and we drove out to the car park of the Shanty pub. The breeze had picked up and whipped my hair into my face. I pulled my jacket tight against my chest and clung to Harry's arm as we negotiated the narrow path to the pub door. I ducked under the low entrance and entered the cosy confines of the Shanty pub with its gorgeous wooden panelling and comfy snugs. The smell of steak and kidney pie mixed with old beer hit my nostrils and reminded me of how hungry I was. I hoped there were still some pies left over from lunch. Harry nudged me and shoved his chin out towards one of the snugs. A young man, the spitting image of Rohan, sat nursing a pint of bitter. Krish Patel. We approached the table and a look of irritation ghosted across his face.

'It's taken,' he said.

'Oh, we're quite happy to share,' said Harry, sitting beside Krish and to all intents and purposes blocking his exit. 'In fact, we'd like to talk to you about a review you left on a blog you didn't own.'

Krish glanced around in panic, but there was no easy escape. Harry was built like a kiosk, and I didn't fancy Krish's chances if he tried to take him on.

'You've no proof it was me,' he said, sneering.

'Nobody else received the original menu,' I said, sitting opposite him and crossing my fingers. 'There were no scallops on the menu on opening night. The only person who knew about the scallop dish, beside Rohan and Kieron, was you.'

He deflated like a burst balloon. He shook his head violently.

'Okay, I wrote the review,' he said. 'I didn't know what would happen that night. I didn't mean for anyone to die because of it. I had planned to post it on opening night to cause the most damage, but the death was nothing to do with me. You've got to believe me. It was a horrible coincidence. I wanted—'

'To wreck your brother's life?' said Harry. 'That's nice.'

'You don't understand. He's the one who's destroying things. Our family for a start. It would kill our parents if they knew about his perversion.'

'You're the only one who thinks it's important,' I said. 'Your mother knows Rohan is gay, and I suspect your father might know too. They don't care anymore. They just want him to be happy.'

'Really?'

'Why don't you ask them?'

A myriad of expressions clashed on his features. He took a long gulp of beer and the muscles in his jaw worked overtime. Finally, he asked: 'And is he happy?'

'He was. Until you destroyed his dreams. He has found a lovely partner, and they had worked for almost a year building a wonderful restaurant. How long did it take you to destroy it? Ten minutes?' I asked.

'You don't understand. I just wanted him to be normal. He used to be like me when we were younger. He used to fancy girls.'

'He used to pretend to like girls,' said Harry. 'That's different.'

'How could you do this to him? He loves you.'

His eyes widened.

179

'He does? But I ruined him. How can he love me?'

'Maybe you should ask him? He's standing over at the bar with Kieron.'

'But what will I do about the restaurant?'

'I doubt you'll be charged by the police. They're looking for bigger fish to fry. Anyway, Rohan won't ask for you to be charged. Why don't you try apologising and see how it goes?'

'I'm dying for a steak and kidney pie,' said Harry, signalling to Rohan to come over. 'Why don't we order one at the bar?'

We left Krish looking for answers in his pint as Rohan and Kieron walked over to him. I saw Rohan reach into his pocket and drop a photograph on the table. Krish picked it up and gazed at it. Then he reached out to Rohan. I pretended to read the menu, but Harry noticed my bright eyes. He shook his head.

'Softy,' he said.

Chapter 30

I lay in bed beside Harry that night, full of steak and kidney pie, and thanked my lucky stars I found such a kind and tolerant man. I had assumed he would be supportive of Rohan and Kieron, and their hopes and dreams, and was not disappointed. With Harry's background in the army, this was not a given. I've never been prouder than seeing him embrace them both, and promise we'd help them get the Surfusion open again. Krish seemed in awe of this Alpha male's attitude to his brother Rohan. I hoped he could learn to be more tolerant in future, at least of his own flesh and blood.

'Are you still awake?' said Harry, his eyes flicking open. 'I know you are. I can feel you thinking. What's on your mind?'

Unwilling to vouchsafe my thoughts on his modern masculinity, I went instead for a believable topic.

'Besides Gladys Fitch, maybe Leanne, and definitely Alan Miller, who knows what the perpetrator looks like?'

Harry chuckled.

'Okay, I'll play. His mother?'

'Hilarious. I'm serious.'

Harry rolled over and supported his head on his elbow.

'Well, he bought the burner phone somewhere. Maybe the person who sold it remembers him.'

'We don't know where he bought it. That doesn't help.'

'He got that tattoo somewhere.'

'Same problem. It must be someone we've already talked to.'

'Go back to the beginning and work forward. Who did we see first?'

I racked my brains for an answer. The night of the opening seemed light years into the past. And then it came to me.

'The fancy dress shop.'

'Ah, but that's how we got Alan Miller's name when I spotted it in the register.'

'That's true. But what if it wasn't Miller who rented the cloak? The owner said the man paid with cash. That sounds pretty suspicious to me in this day and age. Perhaps he didn't want to use a card.'

'I often pay with cash. Am I suspicious?'

'No, just old. Younger people pay with their phones or their cards, not with cash.'

'Thanks a bunch. The owner might remember what the man who hired the cloak looked like. Or have CCTV of the transaction,' said Harry. 'Do you fancy doing a recce down there tomorrow morning?'

'Is the Pope a Catholic?'

The next morning, we got dressed and drank a quick cup of tea before jumping in the Mini and drove back to the costume hire shop in time for it to open.

The owner recognised us and sighed.

'It's Vera and her sidekick,' he said. 'What now?'

'We're sorry to bother you, but this is important. The man who hired the cloak from you may have been responsible for the death of a young man in a restaurant opening a few weeks ago.'

'A death? You didn't tell me that last time.'

'We didn't know. Is there any chance you can remember what he looked like, the guy who hired the cloak?'

'I remember him being odd. He had a hoodie on and skulked about like a criminal.'

'Do you have CCTV?' said Harry.

'Yes, it's backed up on the computer. We can have a look if you like.'

'Really? That would be wonderful.'

He sniffed.

'I don't know why you didn't tell me in the first place. I might have remembered something then.'

'I'm sorry. We didn't know what was going on at the time.'

'Give me a minute. The cloak with the red lining, wasn't it? I doubt I'll ever get it back.'

He looked through the register and found Alan Miller's name and the date. Then he teed up the CCTV on his computer and ran through the day at high speed. He grunted several times and rewound the feed, but then continued. Finally, he swung the screen around to us.

'This is him. I'm sure of it.'

We watched mesmerised as a man in a hoodie appeared at the counter carrying the cloak. He kept his face turned down so it could not be seen on camera. We reviewed the feed several times, but we never glimpsed it. The man was not Alan Miller, though. He was slimmer and a few strands of dark lank hair escaped from the hoodie, nothing like Miller's thatch of brown hair. Then I noticed a tattoo on his right forearm as he reached out to pay. I held in a gasp. Harry saw it too.

'Look,' he said, pointing at the screen.

'Can you freeze the screen when he stretches his arm out, please?' I said.

'Is it the tattoo?' asked the owner. 'Now that's genuine detective work. I feel like I'm on Murder She Wrote. My wife loves that. I can print it out if you want.'

He ran the feed frame by frame until we had the clearest possible view of the tattoo, then he pressed print and a copy of the screen chugged out of the cheap printer beside the computer. He handed it to me.

'What do you think?' he said. 'Any good?'

'Bloody marvellous,' said Harry.

'Um, do you have 1920s outfits for hire?' I said.

'Is this for the investigation?'

'No, something else I'm planning.'

'I've got an entire load in the warehouse.'

'Will you give me your card? I want to run an idea past somebody and your costumes could be perfect for it.'

'Sure. A favour for a favour, huh? I like that.'

'Thank you,' said Harry. 'We're really grateful.'

'You'll let me know how it goes down,' said the man. 'My wife will be so excited I'm in a murder investigation.'

'Of course,' I said.

As we were leaving, Harry turned around and said, 'Just one more thing…'

I thought the man would burst with happiness.

'Colombo,' he said. 'My favourite.'

Chapter 31

My heart started hammering as we left the costume hire shop and didn't slow down on our way to Second Home. I found it hard to concentrate on the road and Harry kept having to remind me to stick to the speed limit.

'Sorry. I'm so excited. This could be the breakthrough we've been waiting for.'

'The only breakthrough we'll have is through the windscreen if you keep driving like a maniac. Slow down. More haste, less speed.'

He was right of course. It didn't stop me from feeling resentful. I was still in television cop mode, and driving under the speed limit did not match my aspirations. I reined in my boy racer attitude and tried to do breathing exercises until we neared Second Home. Luckily, I could park quite close to the shop, and we trotted down the street together, grinning with excitement.

'And where have you two been?' said Mouse. 'I don't approve of this skiving from work.'

'We have news,' I said, waving the printout in his face.

'What is it?' he said, grabbing it and staring hard at the picture. 'Oh my goodness.'

He shot upstairs and I could hear him rifling through his bag before he almost tumbled back down again.

'Look,' he said, thrusting another almost identical picture into my face.

He had blown up the picture given to us by Gladys. The tattoo was not clear in his picture, but even the fuzziness of the image could not disguise the fact it was the same tattoo.

'That's either an astonishing coincidence,' said Harry. 'Or we finally cracked the case.'

'Not quite,' I said. 'The same man may be involved in all the moving parts, but we have no idea who he is yet.'

My mobile phone pinged, and I took it out of my bag. A message from Grace asking if Harry and Mouse could help her deliver some heavy furniture as Max had gone to London, and the client needed it straight away. Harry nodded and slapped Mouse on the shoulder.

'Back to the real world,' he said. 'We'll return soon. Don't solve the case without us.'

They left laughed and joked. I sat behind the counter, trying to calm down after the excitement of the morning. The door of the shop opened and Ghita entered. I could tell from the slumped posture that all was not well in Ghitalandia.

'Well, hello stranger,' I said. 'You are just in time for my daily offer of a free cup of tea and a slice of your own home baked cake.'

'Oh, yes, please. I need a sugar boost. I'm feeling left out and droopy.'

'Have Rohan and Kieron made up, then?'

'Made up? They're practically conjoined. I can't get a word in edgeways.'

'How are preparations going for re-opening?'

'Not well. We can't agree on a plan yet.'

'Come upstairs. I may have an idea. I'm just waiting to speak to somebody about it.'

I took the print-outs of the tattoo images upstairs with me and left them on the window seat. Then I made a pot of tea and cut us two pieces of mochaccino cake. Instead of sitting at our customary table, Ghita headed for the window seat and moved the print-outs so she could sit down. As I carried the tray over, I noticed she had frozen in position, staring at the clearer print-out with her mouth open.

'Are you okay?' I asked.

'This tattoo,' she said, pointing. 'I'm almost sure I've seen it before.'

'Where did you see it? It's really important.'

'I'll be back.'

She stood up again and ran down the stairs. I heard the bell clang as she left. Shaking my head at her sudden departure, I poured myself a cup of tea and nibbled the delicious cake. Then I shut my eyes and enjoyed the sugar rush. Before long, I heard the door open again and the patter of Ghita's tiny feet running up the stairs. Her face glowed crimson with triumph and she panted over to me, waving an old photograph.

'Look. There it is. You see his arm?'

The photograph showed a younger Kieron with another young man standing behind him, his arms wrapped around Kieron's chest. Sure enough, an identical tattoo could be seen on his right forearm. But that wasn't all. I recognised the second young man as Leonard Black, or at least the man who called himself by that name when he had a coffee in my shop. The world seemed to slow to a stop for an instant. I remembered Black's demeanour and sneering attitude toward Surfusion. I should have noticed when he commented that Miller was rather young to have a heart attack. How did he know if they hadn't met? No wonder he didn't want to be interviewed by George. Ghita cleared her throat, and I recognised her method of forcing me back to planet Earth. I nodded.

'I see it. I think you're right. They're the same. Do you know what the young man with Kieron is called?'

'It's his ex-boyfriend, Jason Hunter. The one before Rohan. There was a massive bust up and Jason had his heart broken. Kieron told Rohan he had thrown away all his photos of Jason, but I found this hidden in a drawer in the kitchen. I guess he couldn't bear to part with it.'

'He's the real Leonard Black, if there is such a thing,' I said. 'Or at least Leonard Black is really Jason Hunter. He must have planned the sabotage of Surfusion to get back at Kieron and Rohan.'

'That's a big jump from a couple of fuzzy photographs. How can you be sure?'

'I might have proof right here in the café. Unless I'm mistaken, I have his fingerprints on a cup.'

Chapter 32

It didn't take me long to find Leonard Black's coffee cup, still snug in its Ziplock bag at the back of the cupboard. I took it out and showed it to Ghita.

'Where on earth did you get that?' she said.

'I noticed him looking in the Surfusion window after it shut down. He told me his name was Leonard Black and came here for a coffee. I'm not sure why, but I thought there was something dodgy about him.'

'How long has it been there?'

'A couple of weeks.'

'I don't think it can be used as evidence. You didn't have a warrant.'

I couldn't help but laugh.

'I thought I was supposed to be Jessica Fletcher, not you. Where did you hear that?'

'You're not the only one who knows stuff. I watch true crime on television all the time.'

'You're right. It can't be used as evidence, because he didn't commit a crime in the café, but I still think it will be useful. Joe Brennan can compare it with the prints he already has in the system and identify him as the person who left them on the prawn box and the burner phone chip.'

'How will they charge him?'

'They'll have his name, so they can interview him about his connection to the sabotage. Then they can link everything together.'

'Do you want me to mind the shop for you while you take the cup to the station?'

'That would be great. Can I have the photograph too please? I'll make sure it's not lost.'

'I've a feeling Kieron might not want it anymore after this.'

'You might be right.'

I placed the Ziplock, the printouts and the photograph into my handbag with great care and set out for the station. My mind whirred as I walked along the High Street. I realised Leanne had not resurfaced yet, as far as I knew. Could she have a clue we needed to nail Jason Hunter? I stopped at the doors of Boots the Chemist and texted Mouse, asking for news before heading for the station steps. Sally Wright looked up as I entered.

'George's not in, you know.'

'That's okay. I actually wanted a quick word with Joe Brennan, if that's all right?'

'With Joe? Okay, give me a second.'

She dialled through to him and he came out to reception almost immediately.

'What can I do you for?' he said.

'Um, well, actually, I need a favour.'

'A small favour, or a large favour?'

'A fingerprint check, so only a small favour.'

Joe raised an eyebrow as I removed the Ziplock from my handbag.

'I've a feeling I've seen that mug before.'

'You might have, but I have good reason to believe I've identified the saboteur who caused Alan Miller's death and wrecked Rohan and Kieron's business.'

'Is this a gut feeling? You know how George hates gut feelings.'

'No. I have evidence right here with me I can show you.'

I patted my handbag. He held up his hand.

'Whoa, Hermione, keep your wand sheathed. George will be back soon. Why don't we see if we can lift a print for checking and put it through the Livescan?'

I grinned.

'Now you're talking.'

We walked through the office to Flo's lab, where we found her bent over a thick report. She looked up as we entered and smirked.

'You two look like a pair of naughty school children about to pull a prank. Am I going to get in trouble again?'

'I'm afraid so,' said Joe. 'But if you'd rather read that door stop, I'll understand.'

She snorted.

'I'd prefer to scoop out my eyeballs with a spoon than read this, so you're in luck. What do you need?'

'Can you lift the fingerprints from this mug?' I said.

'Is there a chain of evidence for it? I don't recall us using Ziplock bags in forensics.'

'It will not be used in evidence. It's confirming the identity of a suspect. We'll do an official set if he is charged with anything or brought in for questioning.'

'Hm, that's a little irregular, but as long as it's not to be used in evidence, I can do that for you.'

We waited with barely concealed impatience while Flo put on her lab coat and a new pair of latex gloves. She took the bag from Joe, shaking her head, and tipped the cup out onto a clean metal tray under a bright light.

'Ah, yes, I can see them clearly. They shall not escape.'

She dipped her brush into the fingerprint powder and applied it to the surface of the mug before blowing gently to get rid of the excess. Then she applied a piece of tape to the surface and pressed it down gently. She moved a fingerprint card nearer the cup and then lifted the tape slowly before placing it on the card and smoothing it out. I almost passed out I held my breath so long. Then she repeated the procedure several more times before handing the cards to Joe.

'Are you expecting a match?' she said.

'Definitely,' I said.

'Hopefully,' said Joe.

She followed us up to the Livescan room where Joe put the prints onto the scanning surface one by one. Several clear prints appeared on the computer screen.

'Here goes nothing,' said Joe, and submitted them to the AFIS system. 'It shouldn't take a minute. I'm searching the station database first.'

Sure enough. Two matches pinged up on the screen, one of which was mine.

'It wasn't you, was it?' said Flo.

I rolled my eyes.

'Bingo,' said Joe. 'We have a winner.'

'What winner?' said George, who had just entered the room.

He rolled his eyes when he spotted me trying to be unobtrusive in the corner. 'And exactly what are you doing here?'

'It's a long story,' I said. 'Joe's not to blame. I think I know who the saboteur is, and his fingerprints just confirmed it.'

'Do you have a name?'

'Jason Hunter.'

'Who on earth is Jason Hunter?'

'I was just coming to that.'

'Maybe we should go to the interview room? We don't need you, Joe, thanks.'

Joe's expression nearly made me laugh. I made a phone sign to him as I disappeared into George's office.

'Okay, Tan. What's this all about? Wasting police time is a crime, you know.'

I took the printouts of the tattoos out of my bag and smoothed out on his desk.

'And what are these?'

'One of these photographs was taken on the night of Surfusion's opening from an upstairs window of the flat opposite. It shows a tattoo on the right arm of the driver. The other is from the counter of the costume hire shop. Somebody with an identical tattoo hired the cloak worn by Alan Miller.'

'Can you give me the names and addresses of the people who supplied this information? I'll send Joe round to verify the source and establish a chain of evidence.'

'Of course. I'll text them to you right away.'

'You can do that in a minute. What do the photographs of a tattoo have to do with the fingerprints on the burner phone and the prawn box?'

'The tattoo belongs to Kieron's jilted ex-boyfriend, Jason Hunter. Here's a photograph of them together in better times.'

George gazed at the photograph, and I saw recognition dawn in his eyes.

'That's Leonard Black. He was at the Vintage with you.'

'Exactly. The fingerprints I brought in today were on the coffee cup he left behind in my café.'

'The one I told you not to keep?'

I couldn't look him in the eye, but I nodded my head in affirmation. He groaned and rubbed his forehead.

'You know we can't use it in evidence?'

I grunted.

'Where does this man Hunter live?'

'I have no idea. He hasn't been seen since he came to the Vintage as far as I know.'

'I'll have a chat with Kieron. We'll find Hunter and bring him in for questioning. Do me a favour and stay well away from him. He's likely to get dangerous if cornered.'

'I promise.'

'I should thank you. This is the piece of the jigsaw we were lacking. But I'm too annoyed. Go home.'

'Yes, George.'

I left the station jubilant despite George's refusal to celebrate our win. The police would pick up Jason Hunter, we would refloat Surfusion, and everything would go back to normal. Then my phone pinged, and I broke into a trot.

Chapter 33

I did my best to run all the way, but I had to slow to a walk when I got a bad stitch. Mouse waited for me at the door of the shop, his face pale. He gave me a hug and then showed me his phone. I read the message Leanne had sent him. A short, panicked missive, pleading for help.

'Where is she?'

'She's at the pier.'

'Where's Harry?'

'He's circling in the van. We couldn't find a parking space.'

'Text him and tell him we're waiting for him at the door.'

'What's going on?' said Ghita, who I had forgotten about. 'Did you show George the photograph? What did he say?'

'Jason Hunter is now the prime suspect, but please don't tell anyone yet. George's dealing with it and we don't want to alert Hunter.'

'But why don't we ask Kieron where he is?'

'You're not to get involved. It's far too dangerous and George will blow a gasket.'

'But where are you going now then, if it's so perilous? Why can't I come?'

'There's no room in the van, and we're only going to pick up Leanne. Why don't you lock up the shop, and then go to the Grotty Hovel and meet us there? I'll give you the keys.'

'Will you tell me everything? I'm the one who found the photograph. George would still be stuck without me.'

'Everything, I promise. Take the keys.'

She pouted.

'And feed Hades, or he may try to eat you.'

This made her smile.

'See you soon,' she said. 'Please be careful.'

'We've got Action Man with us. We'll be fine.'

Harry came around the corner, and Mouse and I got into the van.

'Where are we going to park?' I said.

'You've got a point. Maybe we can leave it in the Travelodge car park?'

Luckily, Harry's friend Dave was on duty and let us dump the van and sprint through the hotel and down the pier. I felt glad of my new lungs post giving up smoking as we cantered down the boards of the pier.

'Where is she?' I asked Mouse.

'Hiding in the penny arcade.'

We entered the arcade, breathing heavily like gamblers desperate for our fix. It took me a few seconds to get used to the weird lighting. The machines were lit up and flashing with constant jangling and pinging sounds. The rest of the low-ceilinged room had dim lighting and plenty of places a slim young woman could be hiding. Harry headed behind one row of machines and Mouse down the other. I walked down the central aisle checking out the people playing the games. Shouts of triumph and disappointment punctuated the stream of electronic noises. The sound of tokens dropping in a shower indicated somebody had won big. For a minute, I forgot what I was doing there and longed to try my luck with the slots. Then I thought I saw Leanne and tapped her on the shoulder, but it was an aggressive stranger who accused me of putting her off and losing her money. I didn't dare contradict her, merely apologised and moved on.

A shadow slipped past on my right. I spun around, but couldn't see anybody behind the penny fall machine. The flashing lights made me feel disoriented. I tried to check behind the machine, but only saw Mouse looking in a broom cupboard.

'Where is she?'

'I don't know. She won't answer my texts.'

A piercing shriek rang out, and I spotted Leanne at the far end of the arcade, running out of the side door. I tried to follow her, pushing my way along the aisle, trying not to be rude, but desperate to follow her. Ahead of me, I saw somebody follow her out. Harry burst into the aisle, covered in dust.

'Who screamed?' he said.

'Leanne. She just ran out of the top door, followed by somebody. I'm trying to get there but…'

I gesticulated to the crowd of people. Harry puffed out his chest and roared, 'Get out of the way'. The throng parted like the Red Sea and we ran down the centre, picking up Mouse on our way. We emerged blinking back onto the pier and looked around, trying to spot Leanne.

'There she is,' said Mouse.

Leanne had been backed up against the railings at the end of the pier by a slim young man with a hoodie pulled over his head. When she spotted Mouse, she yelled for help. The man turned around, and I glimpsed his face. Jason Hunter. I started running towards them with Harry and Mouse. Hunter's aggressive expression turned to one of alarm. He shoved Leanne hard so that she fell over the railing, but held on to it and prevented herself from falling into the waves. She screamed in terror. Harry ran to grab her hands and stop her from falling. Hunter took his chance to run away back down the other side of the pier. Mouse turned to run after him.

'Leave him!' shouted Harry, lifting the whimpering Leanne back onto the right side of the railings. 'The police will pick him up.'

Leanne fell into Mouse's arms, crying with relief. It took several minutes for her to calm down, but her legs looked wobbly. Mine were also quaking after all the running I had done.

'Why don't we go into the café and have a pot of tea or something stronger?' I said.

'Good plan,' said Harry.

Mouse put his arm around Leanne and gently guided her inside. We went upstairs to the mezzanine where we sat at one table looking out to sea. Leanne's colour had returned a little, but she still glanced around in pure terror, obviously afraid Hunter might return.

'He's gone,' said Harry. 'He won't get past me. You can relax.'

'Was he the man who came to your flat?' I asked.

'I should have told you about him before,' said Leanne. 'I didn't know who to trust.'

'Told us what?' I said.

'He's the man who delivered the box of prawns to the restaurant, but that's not the first time I saw him. He came to Surfusion about a week before the opening and had a massive row with Kieron in the kitchen. Kieron sent me out when he turned up, but I heard them screaming at each other.'

'Did you hear what they said?'

'No. But when he came back on opening night with the box of prawns, he said they had made up, and he had brought them as a favour because Kieron told him he didn't have enough for the opening night. I didn't want to tell you, because I felt so stupid, and they were in my father's prawn box, so I suspected nothing. And, well, it's my fault that poor man died.'

She began to weep.

'It's not your fault. There was no way of knowing he would have an allergic reaction to the prawns. Lots of people had ceviche, and they were all fine, including me. Why did he come after you?'

'He realised you were getting close to the truth, and he didn't want me to tell you what really happened. I swore I wouldn't snitch on him, but he didn't believe me. I think he intended to get rid of me.'

'He nearly managed,' said Harry.

'You're safe now,' said Mouse. 'You can come home with us, can't she?'

'Of course. But first you have to call your mother. She's frantic with worry about you. And your sister.'

When we had all calmed down, we walked back along the pier and into the car park. Leanne did not get into Harry's van.

'I'd rather go back to my flat,' she said. 'My sister is there. We'll be perfectly safe with the door locked. I'll take a taxi to the door.'

'Are you sure?' I said.

'Quite sure.'

We couldn't persuade Leanne to come with us, so Mouse hailed a taxi and went home with her instead. I decided not to take any chances. I sent a text to George telling him what had happened and where Leanne had gone. I suggested he put an officer on the door of her building, just in case. Harry and I went back to the Grotty Hovel where the smell of curry had escaped under the front door and permeated the air of the street. We entered a cloud of heavenly aromas to find Ghita at the stove stirring a pot of chicken tikka masala.

'Ah, you're just in time. This is a new recipe I'm developing for the Surfusion opening. I need you to try it.'

'Twist my arm,' said Harry.

Chapter 34

The next morning, I got up early as I could not sleep. The sunlight tempted me downstairs to the back door where I sipped a cup of tea and watched Hades frolic in the brambles. He showered himself with petals from the bramble flowers and stalked off in a sulk when I laughed at his impromptu wig. My mobile phone vibrated in my pocket and I wondered who could be ringing so early. George. Honestly, who was awake at this hour?

'Tan, it's me.'

'So I see. Is there a fire?'

'Not yet, but I thought you needed to know that we haven't picked up Jason Hunter yet. We put uniform in a car outside his house last night, but he didn't come home. Can you let the Surfusion lot know so they can be vigilant? I've told the lad outside Leanne's house.'

'No problem. Is there anything we can do?'

'Leave it to us, Tan, please.'

After sending out a round-robin, I swigged down the rest of my tea and went upstairs to get dressed. Harry muttered something I didn't hear, and I kissed his bald dome.

'Stay in bed, sweetheart. Ghita will open the shop. I'll be back later.'

I had not told anyone what I intended to do and even as I got into the car, the wisdom of my plan diminished as I got closer to Tarton Manor House. I lowered the window and let the early summer breeze stream through the car. The scent of honeysuckle, new mown grass and cow dung drifted through and faded out again as I drove the winding lanes to the hotel. Memories of poor Sharon and her untimely demise threatened to intrude, but I dismissed them as quickly as the less pleasant smells. George and Helen were almost a perfect match, and the fates work in funny ways. No wonder the Romans thought the gods were laughing at us.

Tarton Manor House had begun life as a large Georgian rectory, but the addition of various wings and annexes had converted it into a handsome if wonky building of much charm. The hotel was bathed in sunlight when I arrived. The weekend guests had not yet turned up, so the car park had plenty of spaces. I spotted Roz's cousin, Dermot, weeding in the flower beds skirting the main building and gave him a cheery wave, which he reciprocated. The main hall had not yet heated in the sunlight and the hairs on my arms stood on end as I entered its chilly grandeur.

'Can I help you?' said a voice, and I turned around to find the concierge standing behind me.

'Yes. I'd like to speak to Lydia Sheldon, please. She's expecting me.'

'Miss Bowe? I remember you. You're a colleague of DI Antrim's, aren't you?'

'We have worked together occasionally.'

'Mrs Sheldon is in the tearoom. Please go straight through.'

'Thank you.'

Lydia had her laptop open and her head down as I entered. I heard her mutter to herself as she wrestled with whatever problem had arisen on her screen.

'Hi there,' I said. 'Long time no see.'

'Tanya!'

She jumped up and gave me a hug of genuine pleasure. I felt a prickle of pride as we both knew I had restored her to her rightful ownership of Tarton Manor House; a debt that could not be repaid. However, I hoped it meant she would at least consider my hare-brained scheme before dismissing it. All my conviction had drained away on the journey to the hotel, but I would plough on regardless.

'How lovely to see you looking so well.'

'If by that you mean tired and irritable, you've got it in one,' she said. 'Business is not booming the way I hoped. It's rather a slog to tell you the truth.'

An opening if ever I saw one.

'I'm sorry to hear that, but I have a proposition for you. The idea seemed infallible until I drove here, but now I'm feeling foolish for even coming here.'

Lydia closed her laptop.

'Start at the beginning,' she said.

I told her the sorry tale of Surfusion's birth and instant collapse, missing out the details of the police investigation which would not come to court for months. Her eyes widened and her brows lifted and fell in amazement and alarm.

'Let me get this straight. This superb creation had its legs cut from under it on opening night as an act of revenge? How awful, but how fabulous too. It's like an Agatha Christie novel.'

'It is extremely similar, almost to the point of cliché. The problem is that the owners need to relaunch, but they can't imagine how to do it successfully.'

'Is that where I come in?'

I grinned.

'Exactly. When I got involved with the murder investigation here at the hotel, the manager, Tim Boulting, took an almost ghoulish delight in having a murder associated with the hotel.'

'That sounds about right. The man's a horror story all to himself.'

'Well, I'm pretty sure he meant it as a joke, but at the time his callous attitude stunned us. He wanted to treat the tragedy as a money-making venture for the hotel.'

'Don't tell me. He planned to charge for murdering unwanted spouses.'

'Not quite. He mentioned organising weekends for people who were interested in staying in a hotel where a genuine murder had taken place.'

'Killer weekends?'

She leaned forward, her expression alert. I ploughed on.

'I think our horrified reaction may have put him off, but...'

'But you've had an idea? Oh, I totally get it. You've no idea how many people who come to stay at the hotel are interested in the death of poor Sharon. I think some of them choose the hotel for that reason.'

'You do? It's just that I know how many people are fans of murder mysteries and I wondered if we could combine forces to offer them something.'

'Something gruesome? How true crime can you get? I think it's a fabulous idea.'

'Not gruesome, exactly. But more factual for mystery geeks.'

'What's the programme you suggest?'

'I thought guests could arrive at Tarton Manor House on a Friday night and have dinner and maybe a talk about the murder in the hotel. Then on Saturday, a tour of all the important places in the hotel relating to the murder. Your staff could give brief talks about the clues and how they fitted together. Then after lunch they could visit Seacastle and the pier and so on, before going to Surfusion for a talk and a delicious dinner.'

'What about having the same menu as on the night of the murder?'

I found her enthusiasm a little shocking, but I went with it.

'I don't see why not. We could do a pilot weekend with special prices first and if it came off, you could run one once or twice a month.'

'And where do you come in?'

'Oh, I don't. You'd have to talk to Rohan and Kieron.'

'Aren't they the men who catered for Sharon's wedding? I am always being accosted by people who want to know how to get hold of them.'

'Really?' I said.

She blushed.

'I'm sorry. I should have contacted you before now. We work in such a competitive market. I was loath to encourage people to eat elsewhere.'

'I can understand that, but if you work with them, you can both benefit.'

She sat back in her chair. I could almost see the ideas whirling above her head.

'Do you want to work on a proposal?' I said, unwilling to disturb her train of thought.

'What? Oh, yes. Leave it with me. Have you got an email?'

'Yes, or you can send it to my Dropbox.'

'Text it to me.'

She stood up. I knew she wanted me to leave.

'I've got to go,' I said. 'I'm very busy today.'

She laughed.

'I'm sorry. I'm so excited, I didn't even offer you a cup of coffee.'

'That's okay. I have my own café above my vintage shop, Second Home. It's almost opposite Surfusion, if you want to meet the boys upstairs.'

'Wonderful. I'll be in touch as soon as I can put something together. This is going to be fantastic.'

Chapter 35

I came back to Seacastle feeling elated by the result of my meeting. The countryside seemed even more luxuriant and leafy on my way home, and I could hear the birdsong loud over the noise of my engine. I texted ahead to Mouse who greeted me at the counter of Second Home with a delicious latte. When I tried to take it from him, he pulled it out of my reach.

'I'll only give it to you if you tell me where you were.'

'Tarton Manor House.'

'What on earth were you doing there?'

'I have a plan for generating a buzz around Surfusion once it opens again.'

'Can I know what it is?'

'Not yet. I need to talk to Rohan and Kieron first. If they agree, I'll tell you about it. How's Leanne doing by the way?'

'Still shaken. George asked her down to the station to give a statement with her mother in tow.'

'Maybe they'll repair their relationship. It's a pity they're estranged.'

'I don't know how I survived without one for so long.'

I beamed at him.

'You're stuck with me now, anyway. Do you want to help me unpack the stock at the back of the shop?

There's another box of those cool lampshades left over from the seventies.'

'Okay. Finish your coffee and I'll put the boxes out.'

I took out my phone and saw that Ghita had sent a message to our WhatsApp Fat Fighters group advising us of a class the following day. Most of the group had already answered in the affirmative, and I did too. I couldn't wait to see everyone and do something different after the stress of the last few weeks. I looked up to see Rohan and Kieron arriving at Surfusion across the street. They were holding hands, so I judged their mood to be good.

'I'll be back in a minute. I'm just going across the road to talk to Kieron and Rohan about something.'

'Is it anything to do with your mission this morning?'

'It might be.'

'Are you going to tell me about it after you talk to them?'

'Maybe, if you empty the boxes by the time I get back.'

'Hm. I'm not sure that's a good deal.'

'Take it or leave it. I'll be back soon.'

I crossed the street without looking, such was my concentration, and a furious driver screeched to a halt and sounded his horn at me. I waved him an apology and entered the Surfusion, wiping my brow in relief.

'Are you suicidal too?' said Kieron.

I guffawed.

'I blame you. My entire brain is dedicated to this investigation. I completely forgot to check the way was clear. Did you speak to George today?'

'Yes, he called to let us know Jason Hunter had slipped through their fingers,' said Rohan.

'Are you worried about him turning up here?'

'Not really. He'll be in hiding for now. We can't let our lives be ruined by this deranged man. We're going to reopen Surfusion and get on with our lives,' said Kieron.

'I'm glad you said that, because I had a meeting this morning that might interest you.'

'What sort of meeting?' said Rohan.

'I went to Tarton Manor House and spoke to the owner, Lydia Sheldon. She told me people are constantly complimenting your catering at Sharon's wedding.'

'At least we didn't kill her too,' said Kieron.

'That's not funny,' said Rohan. 'What else did she say?'

'We discussed the possibility of organising murder mystery weekends for mystery nerds, which could include a visit to Surfusion.'

'You want people to associate the restaurant with a murder? How's that going to help?' said Rohan.

'No, that's not it,' said Kieron. 'She's suggesting we include a dinner with Tarton Manor House's murder weekends from time to time.'

'Exactly. People would get a talk about the apparent murder and details of the case. It's such a fascinating story. They'd love it.'

'Sabotage, jealousy, mistaken identity. It has all the elements of a spellbinding story,' said Kieron.

'You could run a pilot weekend and see how popular it is before you commit.'

'What about the other days in the month?' said Rohan. 'One or two nights a month wouldn't pay the bills.'

'Just run the restaurant as usual. I have a feeling you'd get many repeat visitors from the murder weekends once they've tried your food. You've also got all those new posh residents from Brighton desperate for somewhere high-end to spend all their extra money. Mouse will help you with social media if you need it.'

'I like it,' said Kieron. 'But the least we could do is to speak to Alan Miller's fiancée before trying to profit from the awful thing that happened to him.'

'Absolutely. If she doesn't mind, we could organise some sort of memorial dinner for him as well. Perhaps when we reopen?' said Rohan.

'You should put a picture of him up beside Ganesha in the alcove,' I said.

'Ganesha is gone. All our luck left when he did,' said Rohan.

I shook my head.

'Ganesha is under the counter in Second Home. Ghita brought him there for safekeeping after the tragic death of Miller.'

'Can I have him back?' said Kieron.

'Follow me,' I said.

'And look both ways crossing the street,' said Rohan.

We went back across to Second Home and I ducked behind the counter to grab the statuette of Ganesha. Kieron almost cried when I handed it over. He stroked it with his thumb.

'Ghita is right about a lot of things,' he said.

'She's a clever woman. Don't let your jealousy destroy your wonderful friendship with her. She would make a wonderful mother for your children if you'd let her.'

'Wouldn't it be very complicated?'

'What isn't? My sister is living with my ex-husband. We grow and adapt if we want to be happy.'

'And I've adopted Tanya as my mother,' said Mouse.

'I never thought of it that way,' said Kieron.

'Neither had I. But I find I'm right.'

Kieron left cradling the statuette. Mouse rolled his eyes at me from behind the counter.

'Honestly, I can't leave you alone for a minute. Why haven't you told me about Ghita having a baby for Rohan and Kieron?'

'You're not supposed to know about it. It may be too tricky or they may change their minds. It's not official yet anyway.'

'It will be if Roz ever hears about it.'

'So don't tell Roz.'

'My lips are sealed. But what's the big secret about Tarton Manor House? Can you at least spill the beans on that?'

'Make me another latte and I'll tell you all about it.'

Chapter 36

I pulled up to the church hall just before Ghita's class started. The hall was bathed in the evening sun, making it appear golden. As I entered through the main door and hung my coat up on the cloakroom, the room reverberated with the sound of women chatting and laughing. The musty odour of children's gym classes and floor polish reminded me of my school days. The shiny floorboards squeaked under my feet and evening sunlight streamed through the top windows. I felt as if I was about to go to the school hop again. Ghita had organised a step for each of us, and some of the fitter ladies had stacked two on top of each other. I had no intention of trying that. One step resembled Everest with my fitness levels.

Ghita welcomed us all to her class and beamed at the enthusiastic response. She had plugged in an old compact disc player to provide the music, and put on one of her favourites, 'Now that's what I call music! DISCO', a compilation of 80s dance hits. The minute the first bars of Le Freak blasted out from the speaker I felt all my troubles ebb away. The smiles on the faces of my friends, especially Ghita, who hadn't been in the mood for laughs since the opening of Surfusion, lightened my heart, and to my surprise, my feet. Soon we were all stepping and clapping and singing together. Despite some early stumbles, I soon got into the rhythm as well. The collective energy was infectious. It's a pity you can't bottle that sort of collective joy and give it to people who are unhappy.

For almost an hour we stomped and clapped and danced together, before an apologetic woman knocked on the door and informed us that the anger management group was due to have a meeting in five minutes. A chorus of low-key complaints could not change her mind. We stacked the steps up at the side of the hall and bid farewell to the members of the group who had children waiting at home. Ghita, Joy, Roz, Grace, Helen and I headed for the Shanty where Flo had already arrived and taken our favourite table in the corner. Joy's husband, Ryan, manned the bar while she joined us for a natter. Ryan surveyed the bar from his specially adapted wheelchair, which lifted him up to talk to people so they didn't talk down to him. Ryan and Joy had both had long careers in MI6, careers which were only nominally over. I was the only person who had inside knowledge of this, but rumours were rife. You couldn't keep nipping over to Eastern Europe without inviting gossip in Seacastle, especially with radar ears like Roz's patrolling the sea front.

Once everyone had received their drinks, the first topic of conversation was Ghita's fantastic class, and what fun it had been, which led inevitably to why she had been absent for so long. Grace, who did not have a British reticence for asking tough questions, demanded to know why we had been abandoned for so long. She knew exactly why, but Ghita, who wasn't usually the centre of attention, revelled in her chance and took the stage.

'What do you know about the opening night at Surfusion?' she said.

I had no intention of butting in and remained silent.

'Somebody died,' said Grace.

'Besides that,' said Ghita, pursing her lips.

'Tell us everything,' said Roz. 'Don't miss anything out.'

'I think it would be better if you missed some things out,' said Helen, frowning. 'It's not all public knowledge yet.'

'I'll stop you if you venture into secret territory,' said Flo.

I watched over the rim of my drink as Ghita gave a wonderful, over the top description of the opening night and the aftermath. Her eyes told the story as she recounted the shock, dismay and confusion. Her tale was punctuated by gasps of horror and sympathy. As she came to the end of her tale, I realised she intended to mention Jason Hunter, so I coughed loudly and shook my head. Alarmed, she glanced at me for reassurance.

'We shouldn't jump the gun as regards the police investigation,' I said.

'Oh, yes, I forgot it's not common knowledge. Well, anyway, we're working towards opening Surfusion again on Saturday.'

'Saturday? But that's only three days,' said Roz.

'Come on, Roz. We all know you can spread a rumour all over Seacastle in ten minutes. Surely, you can do something about this?' said Grace.

'I'm sure you meant that as a compliment,' said Roz, pausing for us all to laugh. 'I'll see what I can do.'

'We can all eat there for a start,' said Flo. 'From what I heard; the food is to die for.'

'It's murderously good,' I said.

'Honestly, do you have to make a joke about everything?' said Ghita, pouting.

'Yes, we do,' said Joy. 'That's how we get through troubled times.'

'I sympathise, Ghita. They'd make jokes on their way to hell.'

'Or heaven,' said Grace. 'In my case.'

'I'd probably get lost,' said Roz.

'Just follow the heat,' said Helen. 'You should be good at that.'

'Speaking of gossip,' said Roz.

Everybody turned to her in anticipation.

'You'll have to buy me a drink first.'

'I'll get it,' said Grace. 'Does anyone else want one?'

'I can't. I'm driving,' I said.

'Me too,' said Flo.

'Great. Cheap round,' said Grace, waving her credit card.

When Roz had her drink, she leaned in and spoke in a stage whisper.

'I heard a rumour that a certain reality show is coming to town.'

Ghita squealed in anticipation.

'Which one is it?'

'You'll never guess,' said Roz.

'No, and that's why I bought you a drink,' said Grace. 'Spit it out.'

'Sloane Rangers.'

'Really? Mouse will be ecstatic. He's got such a crush on Daisy Kallis. I think Harry does as well,' I said.

'Ed claims never to watch television, but he fancies her like mad,' said Roz.

'Lock up your husbands, ladies,' said Helen. 'Or your boyfriends.'

'She doesn't strike me as a man killer,' I said. 'She's sort of fragile.'

'As fragile as Mata Hari,' said Grace. 'It's the quiet ones you need to watch.'

'Are they going to record an episode here in Seacastle?' said Flo.

'That's what I heard,' said Roz.

'Maybe we can get them to eat at Surfusion?' I said. 'I wonder if I know anyone on the production team?'

'Could you really organise something like that?' said Ghita. 'That would be unbelievable.'

'No guarantees, but I'll put some feelers out. The production team from Uncovering the Truth broke up and they are now working in loads of different shows. I can't remember if anyone went to Sloane Rangers.'

'You need to get Surfusion floated again first,' said Helen, always the practical one.

'Where will they stay?' said Grace.

'I don't know yet, but trust me, I will,' said Roz.

I could feel a new plan forming in my head. What if the Sloane Rangers came on a murder mystery weekend? It could save both Tarton Manor House and Surfusion at one stroke. I said nothing, though. Maybe I could get work for the local paper again. I visualised my interviews with the cast.

'Tanya to earth. Are you still with us?'

Helen's voice broke through my reverie.

'Yes, sorry, I was miles away.'

'Mars?' said Ghita. 'Because you really were totally gone.'

They all laughed.

'Who wants another drink?' said Flo.

Chapter 37

Rohan and Kieron could not move ahead with the murder weekends dinner without the permission of Alan Miller's fiancée, Susanne Jones. Since they had not yet met her, they tasked me with inviting her down to the restaurant for a meeting. I called her with some trepidation, remembering her fragile state when Harry and I had visited her in London. She answered on the first ring.

'Hello? Tanya?'

'Yes, it's me. How are you?'

'Doing a little better. I had a visit from the police liaison officer the other day, and she filled me in on the case. How are things in Seacastle? Have they reopened the restaurant yet?'

'That's why I'm calling. The owners wondered if you could visit them for a chat. They have an idea for reopening the restaurant, but they want to run it by you first.'

'Oh. Um. I don't know. Although maybe it would be helpful to see where he died. It might give me some closure.'

'Shall I text their number to you?'

'Will you tell them instead? I'd like you to come with me if you could. I'd find it a lot easier that way.'

'Of course.'

'If I travel by train, can you pick me up at the station?'

'When can you come?'

'Would tomorrow morning be okay?'

'I'm sure it would. Just text me the time you will arrive and I'll let the boys know you are coming. By the way, can you bring a nice photo of Alan? We've never seen him without his disguise and the owners would like to know what he looked like.'

'Of course. I have some copies of one of his publicity photographs. I'll bring it with me.'

Rohan became quite emotional when I told him Susanne would come to see them.

'That poor girl. She's so brave. I feel awful even asking her permission to do this. Maybe we should cancel?'

'She wants closure, so why don't we just play it by ear? You don't have to do this to survive, so it won't be the end of the world if she says no.'

The next day, I picked Susanne up at the Seacastle train station. She had worn a simple dress, which hung loose on her frame, and a matching cardigan. She had tied her hair back. Her bright blue eyes radiated sadness, but she smiled when she spotted me drive up in the Mini. I gave her a hug of welcome and then we drove down to the Surfusion. By chance, I managed to park in a nearby street and we made the short walk to the restaurant. As we entered the restaurant, I heard Susanne gasp. She twirled around and around, gazing at the walls and the décor.

'It's so wonderful. Like being underwater. I love the taxidermy fish.'

'Thank you,' said Rohan, coming forward to shake her hand. 'I'm Rohan Patel. And this is Kieron Murphy. We're the owners of Surfusion.'

'I had no idea how beautiful it was. Alan didn't get the chance to tell me.'

She looked around again.

'Where did Alan sit, you know, on that night?'

'Right over here,' said Rohan, taking her arm and leading her to the table.

'May I sit here for a minute?' she asked.

'Of course.'

She sat down and stroked the painted tabletop in a manner that suggested she had conjured up precious memories. We moved to the front of the restaurant and let her have a quiet moment with the spirit of her lost love. She seemed to have left the room completely. After a while, she sighed and came to join us. She spotted Ganesha in the alcove and pointed at it.

'What's that?' she said.

'Ganesha. He's a Hindu deity, known as a creator and remover of obstacles especially for new ventures. We put him here for good luck,' said Rohan.

'Alan didn't do it on purpose, you know. We needed the money. He didn't have any idea his prank would shut down your restaurant.'

'But he did nothing. He died before he could carry out his mission, whatever it was.'

'He didn't? Oh, what a relief. I felt so guilty. Alan loved pranks, but he never considered the danger of one going wrong.'

'We don't blame Alan. Somebody wanted to sabotage our business, and they succeeded. Unfortunately, with tragic consequences for Alan,' said Kieron.

'Can you reopen the restaurant?'

'Technically, yes,' I said. 'The council has given them the all clear.'

'But we're struggling with how to get people to come here after Alan's death.'

'I see,' said Susanne.

'That's why we needed to talk to you. We have been offered an opportunity to be involved in promotional weekends by a local hotel,' said Rohan. 'They're running them for murder mystery geeks, who would come here to dinner and listen to a talk about a murder case. Alan's mysterious death in the restaurant would be an attraction for them, but we were worried about using it to help us get going again.'

Susanne stood up and walked back over to the table where Alan died. She shut her eyes and took a few deep breaths. I worried we had upset her deeply, or worse horrified her with our callous suggestion. She opened them again and a soft smile spread across her features.

'Alan loved mysteries,' she said. 'He had the complete collection of Agatha Christie novels. Since Alan closed your restaurant, perhaps Ganesha is offering a way for him to reopen it?'

'What a fantastic way of looking at it. I'm so happy we can give you closure,' said Kieron, who rushed over to hug her. She did not resist.

Rohan could not speak because he had choked up with sobs.

'You mean you agree?' I said, stunned at the turn of events.

'Yes, he'd like the idea. I know he would. He'd have said we might as well turn disaster into a triumph.'

'We'd like to put a photograph of Alan in a frame and keep it in Ganesha's alcove, if you don't mind,' said Rohan, recovering his voice. 'He can survey the restaurant and help Ganesha bring us success.'

'I have it here.'

She took it out of her bag. The photograph showed a young, handsome man with a big thatch of brown hair smiling at the camera. Kieron took it from her.

'Wow, what a heartbreaker! I can see why you fell in love with him.'

'He was pretty special,' she said. 'We had a lovely time.'

'I'm so sorry he's gone,' said Rohan. 'But I promise we will never forget him.'

'That's settled then,' she said. 'Now cook me something delicious. I'd like whatever Alan had, but without the peanuts.'

Lydia Sheldon came to see the restaurant the next day. As I had hoped, she was charmed by Surfusion and its owners. On my advice, Kieron prepared a tray of amuse-bouche and they welcomed her into the restaurant with a glass of champagne. Afterwards she came over to Second Home, beaming with delight.

'Oh my goodness!' she said. 'The food is absolutely exquisite. I'm not sure I've ever had anything so delicious. Kieron is a genius.'

'I thought you might be impressed,' I said. 'You should've called them before.'

'My mistake,' she said. 'Let's do this.'

Chapter 38

The pilot murder mystery weekend at Tarton Manor House sold out in days, causing joyful consternation up at the hotel and at the Surfusion restaurant. The timetable for pulling off a successful first run with a full house now seemed a little overoptimistic. Lydia Sheldon called all hands to the pump and got stuck in herself, which helped avoid a debacle. On my suggestion, she asked Rohan if they could organise a 1920s mystery dinner with a staged murder, and he came to me for advice. Of course, I had no problem sourcing costumes for the hotel guests or the participants in the show at Surfusion. The bloke at the costume shop had been ecstatic when we hired almost all of his entire stock of 1920s outfits. He had been so enthusiastic we offered him a small part in the subsequent drama with his wife. Rohan and I wrote a short murder mystery which played out over three courses and roped in most of our friends to take part. I fancied myself as an actress and volunteered immediately, as did Roz. Ghita and Mouse agreed to go along with the ruse in their roles as waiters.

We did minimal rehearsing, but the storyline was simple enough, based as it was on an accidental death caused by sabotage. Setting it in the 1920s removed it from the still raw effects of Alan Miller's death. Everyone coming for the mystery weekend would know the background to the re-creation before they arrived. Harry had agreed to play a police inspector and walk the guests through the clues. We would murder the victim with poison rather than anaphylactic shock, to make it more similar to an Agatha Christie story. Kieron and Rohan had a full week to prepare for the dinner, but the days concertinaed together. Ed Murray spent several days at sea catching fresh fish to order, and Kieron did not leave his kitchen until late at night as he prepared the food for the dinner.

Almost before we were ready, the day of the dinner arrived. I opened Second Home for a half day, mostly so Kieron and Rohan could get last-minute coffees and respite at the Vintage. Considering the importance of the dinner, I found them remarkably calm, but Roz remarked they had the aura of condemned men.

'It's all-or-nothing today,' said Harry, as we changed into our outfits. 'I hope I remember my lines.'

'You'll be great,' I said, crossing my fingers.

Mouse went ahead of us to give the glasses one last shine, and then we made our way to the restaurant to meet up with the others. An air of nervous anticipation hung in the air. Rohan gave us a pep talk before the guests arrived, which only increased the tension. As the time for the guests' arrival approached, we spread ourselves out among the tables. Being in costume made it easier to get into character. We were a handsome bunch in our finery. Ghita and Mouse were wearing old-fashioned waiting uniforms, and Rohan sported the outfit of a Maître D. Grace, Helen and Roz and I wore flappers' dresses and wigs, while the men wore dinner jackets. Candlelight added atmosphere to the restaurant and the taxidermy fish loomed out of the darkness, their goggly eyes focussed on the tableau before them.

Then the door to the street opened and the first guests filtered in dressed in their glad rags and gazing around the interior with awe.

'It's like something out of Jules Verne,' said one.

'Twenty thousand leagues under the Sea? My thoughts exactly,' said another.

I elbowed Roz, who grinned at me from under her flapper's wig. Since we were all in costume, people shot nervous glances about the room, unable to pick out the actors. It occurred to me that the guests were almost as nervous as us. I noticed Mouse and Ghita whispering together as the guests took their seats around us. As soon as everyone got seated, Mouse and Ghita came around with trays of amuse bouche and filled eager glasses with prosecco. The appearance and taste of the tasty treats cause groans of pleasure from the diners who eyed the kitchen door in anticipation of the starters. Since most of the guests were programmed to arrive and leave at the same time, Kieron had prepared a fixed-price menu of three courses with three choices for each course, one vegetarian and two fish based. Lydia Sheldon had already sent him a list of orders for the evening and we had also pre-ordered, so he could get all his ducks, or fish, in a row before the dinner started.

Mouse came out of the kitchen with several plates of starters and distributed them to the guests and players alike. Soon the air was thick with exclamations of delight as people tasted their food. I had ordered ceviche again, and it tasted like the sea with pieces of fresh popcorn floating on the surface like fluffy clouds. Suddenly, Ed Murray stood up and grabbed his throat, falling to the floor in dramatic fashion. Roz screamed theatrically and Harry rushed over to the 'body'. He leaned over Ed and shook his head.

'He's dead, I'm afraid. There's foam coming out of his mouth. Somebody poisoned him.'

A loud gasp accompanied this pronouncement as the guests joined in the consternation. Their excitement was catching. I almost forgot we were acting.

'Did anybody see what happened?' said Harry.

'I did,' said Helen, pointing at me. 'That woman put something in his drink.'

'Don't be ridiculous,' I said. 'It was the chef. He poisoned the food. It's obvious.'

My attempt at acting seemed to irritate one diner who pushed his chair backwards and stood up. The blood froze in my veins as I recognised Jason Hunter. What ever possessed him to turn up again? I took a risk and improvised my dialogue.

'What about him?' I said. 'He looks suspicious. We should call the police.'

'But I am the police,' said Harry, giving me a funny look. 'Don't interfere with the investigation.'

Harry went back to his prepared lines, but Hunter went over and stopped him. I saw Rohan go rigid and then grab his phone discreetly from under the counter and send a text.

'That's not what happened at all,' said Hunter, pointing at Rohan. 'This man stole the love of my life. He ruined everything.'

The guests were agog. Obviously, they had no idea the play had gone horribly wrong. I held my breath. Kieron appeared at the kitchen door and his hand flew to his mouth. Hunter turned to face him, his face purple with fury.

'You traitor! How could you leave me for this popinjay?'

Kieron's jaw worked, and he wiped his hands on his apron, leaving a red smear.

'I didn't intend to hurt you,' he said. 'I fell in love and you wouldn't accept it.'

'Why should I? You were mine. I wanted you back. I'd have done anything.'

'And now somebody's dead. How could you do that?' said Rohan.

Hunter shrugged.

'I just wanted to put people off coming to the Surfusion. I didn't know he was going to die. He told me he always carried an EpiPen, so I thought he would just suffer from an allergy and cause a scandal which would damage the restaurant. But now you're going to die instead.'

He shoved Harry out of the way, surprising him and knocking him to the floor. Then he took out a knife and advanced on Kieron with it raised in the air. Before anyone else could react, I heard a cry like a banshee echo through the restaurant. Ghita had reached up to remove Ganesha from the alcove and launched herself through the tables, carrying the statuette in her right hand. Before Hunter could recover from his amazement at this mad vision in a maid uniform, she had clonked him on the head with it. He crumpled to the ground. A shocked silence reverberated through the guests until Harry stood up again and applauded with all his might.

'Bravo,' he said, and I joined in with Roz, cheering and clapping.

At that moment, George and Joe burst through the door and jogged over to the spot where Hunter moaned on the floor.

'What on earth's going on?' said George.

Harry reacted the quickest.

'Oh, there you are, Hargreaves. Take this man down to the cells. He'll hang for this.'

Helen nodded vigorously at George to play along. Joe Brennan helped the still groggy Jason Hunter stand up and put handcuffs on his wrists. They marched him towards the restaurant's exit. The stunned guests joined in the cheering and clapped them out of the door. George bowed, bemused. Joe Brennan gave a wave to the adoring public. Rohan stumbled over and embraced Kieron as if he would never release him. And Ghita?

Well, she stood there with the statuette in her hand, looking astonished with herself as the whole place exploded in applause for her. I rushed over to her and prised Ganesha away from her tight grasp. Then Harry guided her back to her table. She appeared to be in shock. Roz replenished her glass and made her drink. Meanwhile, I replaced the statuette in the alcove beside the photograph of Alan Miller. He had stared out over the proceedings in approval. I could have sworn he winked at me. I shook my head and returned to where Rohan and Kieron still stood clasped together.

'I think it's time for the main course,' I said.

The rest of the evening passed by in a blur. The guests did not seem to realise they had been privy to a real-life drama, toasting Ghita and the police with glee. Their reaction to the food could not have been better. Kieron's dishes were inspired. The blend of spices in the sauces was like a party in my mouth and judging by the expressions on the faces of the clients, they were amazed by the breadth of flavour in their food. Kieron couldn't help sneaking a peep around the door after the main courses came out. His broad grin widened still more as people clamoured to outdo each other in their ecstatic responses. The photograph of Alan Miller gazed down on the scene and I couldn't escape the feeling he had enjoyed the evening.

After the mystery weekend guests filed out, still breathless with excitement about the mystery and the meal, we gravitated to the front of the restaurant where Kieron poured us all a liqueur. We raised our glasses to Rohan and Kieron.

'I've never had such delicious food,' said Harry. 'I should never have doubted you both. You've pulled it off.'

'Did you see how excited they were?' said Helen. 'They had no idea they almost witnessed an actual murder.'

'Ghita saved my life,' said Kieron.

'We'll never be able to repay you,' said Rohan. 'You're a rare treasure.'

'I didn't even know I'd done it until I saw him on the floor. I couldn't let him hurt Kieron.'

'I couldn't believe it when you sprinted across the restaurant and bonked him on the head with that icon,' said Roz. 'I always thought of you as timid. Never again.'

'You're my hero,' said Mouse.

Ghita blushed crimson to the roots of her hair.

Kieron raised his glass.

'Here's to Ghita Chowdhury, a real-life heroine and the future mother of our children.'

I don't think I've ever seen Roz so astonished, but we all cheered and drank to our friend, a small person of massive consequence.

Rohan staggered to his feet and raised his glass.

'And I'd like to toast our friend Tanya Bowe, without whom we would never have been able to reopen. She is brave and stubborn and runs rings around George, and we can never thank her enough for saving our restaurant.'

'Don't forget my partners in crime, Harry Fletcher and Mouse Carter. They are my sounding posts and the loves of my life. I would collapse in a heap without either of them,' I said, trying not to cry.

We walked home along the promenade with Helen. George had not yet reappeared from booking Hunter at the police station, so we walked her to their house two streets over from mine, before returning to the Grotty Hovel. She gave me a tender hug at her front door and whispered that she was proud of me and not to give George a hard time. Harry and Mouse also gave her a hug before we headed home through the quiet streets. Although it was almost midnight, televisions flickered in some of the ground-floor windows, showing not everybody had gone to bed yet.

'I feel like D'artagnan and the two musketeers,' said Mouse. 'Now we lost Helen.'

'I was going for the Great Gatsby,' I said, shaking the fringe at the bottom of my flapper dress.

'You're both delusional,' said Harry. 'I need a cup of tea.'

Chapter 39

The next morning, Harry and I lay side by side like two slugs on a lettuce leaf and snoozed until late. When we woke, we chatted about the success of the mystery dinner despite the unexpected presence of Jason Hunter.

'I can't believe his cavalier attitude to causing poor Alan Miller's anaphylactic shock when he knew about his allergy. Will George be able to charge him with murder?' asked Harry.

'I don't know. I think he used Miller without a thought to the consequences of sending him into shock. It's horrific.'

'Do you think the diners guessed that George and Joe were real policemen?'

'I don't know. Once we started clapping, they copied us, so maybe they preferred not to know the truth.'

'Whatever the explanation, the entire experience bordered on the extraordinary.'

He had a point. People had gone up to Rohan and Kieron to shake their hands and I heard words such as magnificent, delicious, innovative and fabulous leaking from their conversations. Lydia Sheldon would be thrilled and hopefully she would programme more weekends soon. Rohan, with Mouse's help, had printed cards with a message thanking the diners for their custom and asking them to review Surfusion on their favourite sites to help the restaurant relaunch.

'Do you think people will return to the Surfusion?' said Harry.

'I don't know. I hope Jim Swift at the Seacastle Echo will feature them in the review section. Customers may come out of morbid curiosity if nothing else.'

'I can't believe it all came down to a tattoo.'

'Speaking of which, would you come with me and see Gladys this afternoon? We can get her a pretty bunch of flowers and pop in to see her to update her on the investigation like I promised.'

'That's a brilliant plan. Maybe we can roast that shoulder of lamb I got on special offer this evening?'

'Yum. It's a deal.'

We showered and dressed and had a brunch of scrambled eggs and sausages and fried bread, before setting out to buy her the flowers. We settled on a bunch of beautiful purple-blue irises with yellow centres wrapped in sea green cellophane. Gladys took a while to answer the intercom, but her voice went up an octave in delight when I asked if the sleuth was in residence. Gladys received the flowers from Harry with a blush and made a great fuss over finding the right vase for them. She placed them in the centre of the table, where they spread joy around the room. After we were settled, I told her all about the investigation and showed her the picture of Kieron and Jason Hunter with the tattoo on his arm.

'You cracked the case, Gladys,' said Harry. 'Without your photograph we'd still be in the dark about all of this.'

She went pink with pleasure and bit her lip.

'Oh, I found my notes. I had forgotten the decal in the back window of the car. I noticed it even from this far away because the logo is so familiar; The Seagulls.'

'I'll tell George. He'll be thrilled. Miller's girlfriend noticed the decal too, so it all goes in the evidence bucket against Hunter.'

'What an evil man. Imagine taking a chance like that out of jealousy. Poor old Alan Miller.'

We left Gladys in her flat basking in her triumph and gazing at her flowers. I had a feeling we'd be seeing more of her at Second Home. The lamb hit the spot too. Who doesn't love roast lamb and roast parsnips?

The eventual reopening of Surfusion to the public was more low-key than the pilot mystery dinner, but the atmosphere made up for the lack of pizzazz. Ed came up trumps with another fantastic selection of fresh seafood, and Kieron's inspired dishes were mouthwatering and unique. We filled the restaurant despite the reluctance of the dining public to risk a visit. Ghita's parents made her dissolve into tears of joy by turning up, but the biggest surprise of the night came when Rohan's brother Krish appeared with their parents in tow. Rohan's face suffused with joy made me quite tearful. Harry had to lend me his handkerchief when I failed to dig a tissue out of my handbag.

As I observed the different family dynamics, I reflected on the complexity of human relationships and reminded myself of the trite maxim that everyone is dealing with something you don't know about. In our case, most people were dealing with unique generational takes on life. Ghita struggled against her parents' conviction that her life could not be complete without a husband; Rohan's parents trying to persuade him that his choice was the wrong sex; Kieron's mother thought she should come first in his life and demanded he give up everything to move back in with her. Most people's lives are quiet train wrecks.

Although I missed my parents, sometimes I felt relieved they weren't around to criticise Helen for choosing George, and me for losing him. Mouse had had to deal with losing his mother, and having a father for whom he didn't make the grade. The only person free of worries was Hades, and he complained more than anyone, yowling if his breakfast was five minutes late or his basket was not comfy enough. The only thing we all had in common was love.

Harry shook his head at Ghita and Rohan bickering at the till. I don't think he had recovered from seeing Ghita pounce on Hunter. He had been primed to leap in and break up a fight if necessary, but Ghita had beaten him to it. I reached over to grab Harry's hand and he squeezed mine back. The tension went out of his shoulders.

'Let's get out of here,' he said.

'I thought you'd never ask.'

Thank you for reading my book. Please leave me a review if you enjoyed it.

The next in the series – **GRAVE REALITY** –will be out in early 2025. Pre-order by using your phone to read the QR code below.

I am also publishing a Christmas mystery for this series in November 2024. Pre-order **PURRFECT CRIME** by using this QR code with your phone.

Other books

The Seacastle Mysteries - a cosy mystery series set on the south coast of England

Deadly Return (Book 1)

Staying away is hard, but returning may prove fatal. Tanya Bowe, a former investigative journalist, is adjusting to life as an impoverished divorcee in the seaside town of Seacastle. She crosses paths with a long-lost schoolmate, Melanie Conrad, during a house clearance to find stock for her vintage shop. The two women renew their friendship, but their reunion takes a tragic turn when Mel is found lifeless at the foot of the stairs in the same house.

While the police are quick to label Mel's death as an accident, Tanya's gut tells her there's more to the story. Driven by her instincts, she embarks on her own investigation, delving into Mel's mysterious past. As she probes deep into the Conrad family's secrets, Tanya uncovers a complex web of lies and blackmail. But the further she digs, the more intricate the puzzle becomes. As Tanya's determination grows, so does the shadow of danger. Each new revelation brings her closer to a chilling truth. Can she unravel the secrets surrounding Mel's demise before the killer strikes again?

Eternal Forest (Book 2)

What if proving a friend's husband innocent of murder implicates her instead?

Tanya Bowe, an ex-investigative journalist, and divorcee, runs a vintage shop in the coastal town of Seacastle. When her old friend, Lexi Burlington-Smythe borrows the office above the shop as a base for the campaign to create a kelp sanctuary off the coast, Tanya is thrilled with the chance to get involved and make some extra money. Tanya soon gets drawn into the high-stake arguments surrounding the campaign, as tempers are frayed, and her friends, Roz and Ghita favour opposing camps. When a celebrity eco warrior is murdered, the evidence implicates Roz's husband Ed, and Tanya finds her loyalties stretched to breaking point as she struggles to discover the true identity of the murderer.

Fatal Tribute (Book 3)
How do you find the murderer when every act is convincing?
Tanya Bowe, an ex-investigative journalist, agrees to interview the contestants of the National Talent Competition for the local newspaper, but finds herself up to her neck in secrets, sabotage and simmering resentment. The tensions increase when her condescending sister comes to stay next door for the duration of the contest.
Several rising stars on the circuit hope to win the competition, but old stager, Lance Emerald, is not going down without a fight. When Lance is found dead in his dressing room, Tanya is determined to find the murderer, but complex dynamics between the contestants and fraught family relationships make the mystery harder to solve. **Can Tanya uncover the truth before another murder takes centre stage?**

Toxic Vows (Book 4)

A shotgun marriage can lead to deadly celebrations
Despite her reservations, Tanya Bowe, ex-investigative journalist and local sleuth, feels obliged to plan and attend the wedding of her ex-husband DI George Carter. The atmosphere is less than convivial as underlying tensions bubble to the surface. But when the bride is found dead only hours after the ceremony, the spotlight is firmly turned onto George as the prime suspect. A reluctant Tanya is forced to come to George's aid when his rival, DI Antrim is determined to prove him responsible for her death. She discovers the bride had a lot of dangerous secrets, but so did other guests at the wedding. Did the murderer intend to kill, or have an elaborate plan gone badly wrong?

Mortal Vintage
Does an ancient coven hold the key to solving a murder?
Few tears are shed when the unpopular manager of the annual Seacastle Vintage Fair meets a sinister end. But local sleuth Tanya Bowe is thrust into the heart of the investigation when her friend, Grace Wong, finds herself under scrutiny for the murder. When Tanya's investigation uncovers a suspicious death in the same family, all bets are off. She navigates dark undercurrents of greed and betrayal as she uncovers a labyrinth of potential suspects associated with an ancient coven. Nothing is as it seems, and every clue adds extra complications. To solve the case, Tanya must answer one key question. Did someone hate the victim enough to kill her, or was greed the stronger motive?

Grave Reality

When death rewrites the script, a reality show takes a fatal detour

Chaos breaks out in the quiet town of Seacastle when the cast and crew of the hit show Sloane Rangers descend upon the town, stirring up drama both on and off the screen. Local sleuth and former investigative reporter, Tanya Bowe, is brought on board as a consultant, tasked with generating buzz for the local and national press. But she quickly uncovers a tangled web of strained relationships and simmering tensions among the cast. When one of the stars is discovered dead on set, she finds herself at the heart of a murder investigation. To complicate matters, the lead detective is her ex-husband, DI George Carter, who's adamant about keeping her out of his investigation. But Tanya isn't one to sit on the sidelines and she's soon up to her neck in controversy. As the case unfolds, a beloved cast member emerges as the prime suspect, sending shockwaves through Seacastle. With everyone playing a part and secrets buried deep, the murderer remains hidden in plain sight. Can Tanya unravel the truth before she becomes the next victim?

Purrfect Crime – A Christmas Mystery

The purrfect Christmas mystery to keep you up all night.

When preparations for Christmas at the Grotty Hovel are interrupted by the discovery of a body in the back garden, local sleuth, Tanya Bowe, finds herself embroiled in a cold case mystery. The local police are less than enthusiastic about pursuing the case before the holidays, but Tanya can't wait. Then Hades, their rescue cat, goes missing, and all festivities are put on hold as Tanya and her housemates search high and low for their pesky feline. As the hunt for Hades becomes more frantic, Tanya suspects his disappearance may be linked to the body in her garden. Who has kit-napped Hades? Will Tanya find the murderer before the turkey starts to rot?

Other books by the Author

I write under various pen names in different genres. If you are looking for another mystery, why don't you try **Mortal Mission,** written as Pip Skinner.

Mortal Mission

Will they find life on Mars, or death?

When the science officer for the first crewed mission to Mars dies suddenly, backup Hattie Fredericks gets the coveted place on the crew. But her presence on the Starship provokes suspicion when it coincides with a series of incidents which threaten to derail the mission. After a near-miss while landing on the planet, the world watches as Hattie and her fellow astronauts struggle to survive. But, worse than the harsh elements on Mars, is their growing realisation that someone, somewhere, is trying to destroy the mission.

When more astronauts die, Hattie doesn't know who to trust. And her only allies are 35 million miles away. As the tension ratchets up, violence and suspicion invade both worlds. If you like science-based sci-fi and a locked-room mystery with a twist, you'll love this book.

The Green Family Saga

Rebel Green – Book 1
Relationships fracture when two families find themselves caught up in the Irish Troubles.

The Green family move to Kilkenny from England in 1969, at the beginning of the conflict in Northern Ireland. They rent a farmhouse on the outskirts of town and make friends with the O'Connor family next door. Not every member of the family adapts easily to their new life, and their differing approaches lead to misunderstandings and friction. Despite this, the bonds between the family members deepen with time.

Perturbed by the worsening violence in the North threatening to invade their lives, the children make a pact never to let the troubles come between them. But promises can be broken, with tragic consequences for everyone.

Africa Green – Book 2
Will a white chimp save its rescuers or get them killed?

Journalist Isabella Green travels to Sierra Leone, a country emerging from civil war, to write an article about a chimp sanctuary. Animals that need saving are her obsession, and she can't resist getting involved with the project, which is on the verge of bankruptcy. She forms a bond with local boy, Ten, and army veteran, Pete, to try to save it. When they rescue a rare white chimp from a village frequented by a dangerous rebel splinter group, the resulting media interest could save the sanctuary. But the rebel group has not signed the ceasefire. They believe the voodoo power of the white chimp protects them from bullets, and they are determined to take it back so they can storm the capital. When Pete and Ten go missing, only Isabella stands in the rebels' way. Her love for the chimps unlocks the fighting spirit within her. Can she save the sanctuary or will she die trying?

Fighting Green – Book 3

Liz Green is desperate for a change. The Dot-Com boom is raging in the City of London, and she feels exhausted and out of her depth. Added to that, her long-term boyfriend, Sean O'Connor, is drinking too much and shows signs of going off the rails. Determined to start anew, Liz abandons both Sean and her job, and buys a near-derelict house in Ireland to renovate.

She moves to Thomastown where she renews old ties and makes new ones, including two lawyers who become rivals for her affection. When Sean's attempt to win her back goes disastrously wrong, Liz finishes with him for good. Finding herself almost penniless, and forced to seek new ways to survive, Liz is torn between making a fresh start and going back to her old loves.

Can Liz make a go of her new life, or will her past become her future?

The Sam Harris Series (written as PJ Skinner)

Set in the late 1980s and through the 1990s, the thrilling Sam Harris Adventure series navigates through the career of a female geologist. Themes such as women working in formerly male domains, and what constitutes a normal existence, are developed in the context of Sam's constant ability to find herself in the middle of an adventure or mystery. Sam's home life provides a contrast to her adventures and feeds her need to escape. Her attachment to an unfaithful boyfriend is the thread running through her romantic life, and her attempts to break free of it provide another side to her character.

The first book in the Sam Harris Series sets the scene for the career of an unwilling heroine, whose bravery and resourcefulness are needed to navigate a series of adventures set in remote sites in Africa and South America. Based loosely on the real-life adventures of the author, the settings and characters are given an authenticity that will connect with readers who enjoy adventure fiction and mysteries set in remote settings with realistic scenarios.

Fool's Gold - Book 1

Newly qualified geologist Sam Harris is a woman in a man's world - overlooked, underpaid but resilient and passionate. Desperate for her first job, and nursing a broken heart, she accepts an offer from notorious entrepreneur Mike Morton, to search for gold deposits in the remote rainforests of Sierramar. With the help of nutty local heiress Gloria Sanchez, she soon settles into life in Calderon, the capital. But when she accidentally uncovers a long-lost clue to a treasure buried deep within the jungle, her journey really begins. Teaming up with geologist Wilson Ortega, historian Alfredo Vargas and the mysterious Don Moises, they venture through the jungle, where she lurches between excitement and insecurity. Yet there is a far graver threat looming; Mike and Gloria discover that one member of the expedition is plotting to seize the fortune for himself and will do anything to get it. Can Sam survive and find the treasure, or will her first adventure be her last?

Hitler's Finger - Book 2

The second book in the Sam Harris Series sees the return of our heroine Sam Harris to Sierramar to help her friend Gloria track down her boyfriend, the historian Alfredo Vargas. Geologist Sam Harris loves getting her hands dirty. So, when she learns that her friend Alfredo has gone missing in Sierramar, she gives her personal life some much needed space and hops on the next plane. But she never expected to be following the trail of a devious Nazi plot nearly 50 years after World War II ... Deep in a remote mountain settlement, Sam must uncover the village's dark history. If she cannot reach her friend in time, the Nazi survivors will ensure Alfredo's permanent silence. Can Sam blow the lid on the conspiracy before the Third Reich makes a devastating return?

The Star of Simbako - Book 3

A fabled diamond, a jealous voodoo priestess, disturbing cultural practices. What might go wrong? The third book in the Sam Harris Series sees Sam Harris on her first contract to West Africa to Simbako, a land of tribal kingdoms and voodoo. Nursing a broken heart, Sam Harris goes to Simbako to work in the diamond fields of Fona. She is soon involved with a cast of characters who are starring in their own soap opera, a dangerous mix of superstition, cultural practices, and ignorance (mostly her own). Add a love triangle and a jealous woman who wants her dead and Sam is in trouble again. Where is the Star of Simbako? Is Sam going to survive the chaos?

The Pink Elephants - Book 4

Sam gets a call in the middle of the night that takes her to the Masaibu project in Lumbono, Africa. The project is collapsing under the weight of corruption and chicanery engendered by management, both in country and back on the main company board. Sam has to navigate murky waters to get it back on course, not helped by interference from people who want her to fail. When poachers invade the elephant sanctuary next door, her problems multiply. Can Sam protect the elephants and save the project or will she have to choose?

The Bonita Protocol - Book 5

An erratic boss. Suspicious results. Stock market shenanigans. Can Sam Harris expose the scam before they silence her? It's 1996. Geologist Sam Harris has been around the block, but she's prone to nostalgia, so she snatches the chance to work in Sierramar, her old stomping ground. But she never expected to be working for a company that is breaking all the rules. When the analysis results from drill samples are suspiciously high, Sam makes a decision that puts her life in peril. Can she blow the lid on the conspiracy before they shut her up for good?

Digging Deeper - Book 6

A feisty geologist working in the diamond fields of West Africa is kidnapped by rebels. Can she survive the ordeal, or will this adventure be her last? It's 1998. Geologist Sam Harris is desperate for money, so she takes a job in a tinpot mining company working in war-torn Tamazia. But she never expected to be kidnapped by blood thirsty rebels.

Working in Gemsite would never be easy with its culture of misogyny and corruption. Her boss, the notorious Adrian Black is engaged in a game of cat and mouse with the government over taxation. Just when Sam makes a breakthrough, the camp is overrun by rebels and Sam is taken captive. Will anyone bother to rescue her, and will she still be alive if they do?

Concrete Jungle - Book 7 (series end)

Armed with an MBA, Sam Harris is storming the City - But has she swapped one jungle for another?

Forging a new career would never be easy, and Sam discovers she has not escaped from the culture of misogyny and corruption that blighted her field career.

When her past is revealed, she finally achieves the acceptance she has always craved, but being one of the boys is not the panacea she expected. The death of a new friend presents her with the stark choice of compromising her principals to keep her new position, or exposing the truth behind the façade. Will she finally get what she wants or was it all a mirage?

Box Sets

Sam Harris Adventure Box Set Book 2-4
Sam Harris Adventure Box Set Book 5-7
Sam Harris Adventure Box Set Books 2-7

Connect with the Author

About the Author

I write under several pen names and in various genres: PJ Skinner (Travel Adventures and Cozy/Cosy Mystery), Pip Skinner (Sci-Fi), Kate Foley (Irish contemporary), and Jessica Parkin (children's illustrated books).

I moved to the south coast of England just before the Covid pandemic and after finishing my trilogy, The Green Family Saga, I planned the Seacastle Mysteries. I have always been a massive fan of crime and mystery and I guess it was inevitable I would turn my hand to a mystery series eventually.

Before I wrote novels, I spent 30 years working as an exploration geologist, managing remote sites and doing due diligence on projects in over thirty countries. During this time, I collected the tall tales and real-life experiences which inspired the Sam Harris Adventure Series, chronicling the adventures of a female geologist as a pioneer in a hitherto exclusively male world.

I worked in many countries in South America and Africa in remote, strange, and often dangerous places, and loved every minute, despite encountering my fair share of misogyny and other perils. The Sam Harris Adventure Series is for lovers of intelligent adventure thrillers happening just before the time of mobile phones and the internet. It has a unique viewpoint provided by Sam, a female interloper in a male world, as she struggles with alien cultures and failed relationships.

My childhood in Ireland inspired me to write the Green Family Saga (as Kate Foley), which follows the fortunes of an English family who move to Ireland just before the start of the troubles.

I have also written a mystery on Mars, Mortal Mission, inspired by my fascination with all things celestial. It is a science-based murder mystery, think The Martian with fewer potatoes and more bodies.

Follow me on Amazon to get informed of my new releases. Just put PJ Skinner into the search box on Amazon and then click on the follow button on my author page.

Please subscribe to my Seacastle Mysteries Newsletter for updates and offers by using this QR code

You can also use the QR code below to get to my website for updates and to buy paperbacks direct from me.

You can also follow me on Twitter, Instagram, TikTok, or on Facebook @pjskinnerauthor

Printed in Great Britain
by Amazon